I0570564

Detroitopia

Book Two:

Wanted Man

by
Cyrus Vanover

PUBLISHED BY:
Iconic Inkwell

Detroitopia
Part One: After Detroit

Copyright © 2014 Cyrus Vanover

All rights reserved.

No part of this publication may be copied, reproduced in any format, by any means, electronic or otherwise, without the prior written permission of the copyright owner.

This book is a work of fiction. The names, characters, places, and incidents are products of the writer's imagination or have been used fictitiously and are not to be construed as real. Any resemblance to persons, living or dead, actual events, locales, or organizations is entirely coincidental.

Any product names, brands, and other trademarks that may be referred to within this book are the property of their respective trademark holders. Unless otherwise specified, no association between the author and any trademark holder is expressed or implied. Use of a term in this book should not be regarded as affecting the validity of any trademark, registered trademark, or service mark.

ISBN-13: 978-0692243800
ISBN-10: 0692243801

Printed in the United States of America

First Edition: June 2014

10 9 8 7 6 5 4 3 2 1

Be sure to visit the author's web site for updates on new book releases and other exciting things!

www.cyrusvanoverbooks.com

CHAPTER 1

I OPEN MY EYES AND let the world around me slowly come into focus. I'm in a room of some sort, although I can't remember how I got here or why I'm here. A few rays of sunshine are entering the room through a small window at ground level, illuminating the room just enough so that I can see my surroundings. It's not much to look at.

The room is mostly empty, although there is a shelf along one wall with a few boxes on it and a small table at the opposite end of the room. An overcoat hangs on the wall near the door. A thick layer of dust covers the floor and the shelves. And the smell. The room has a strong smell of must combined with the stench of something rotting. It's almost overwhelming and I have the strong urge to open a window to let some fresh air in.

As my eyes continue to adjust to the low light and my surroundings, it all starts coming back to me, like some kind of bad dream made real. I remember Elise resisting the sentry as he tried to force himself upon her. I also remember the dastardly thing I did to the sentry to protect her and how I fled from the other sentry and found refuge in this room. Yes, I remember it all now... unfortunately.

Oh, how I wish I could get a do-over on the events that occurred yesterday. If only I could have arrived at Dr. Bradshaw's home just a few minutes earlier, perhaps none of what transpired would've happened. Perhaps things would have ended up as I imagined them, with Elise and Dr. Bradshaw both being very pleased with my decision to join their rebellion against an increasingly belligerent army of sentry soldiers that makes all our lives miserable. If only. But things didn't exactly go as planned.

I am now a fugitive and have to try to make sense out of all of this. I have to figure out where I'm going to go, what I'm going to do, and how I'm going to live—if it's even possible to have a life at all now. I simply don't know. Sometimes life will throw a huge curve ball at us that we couldn't possibly have seen coming. The only thing we can do when these things happen is to make the best of our circumstances. Still, it's hard to be optimistic considering the position I'm now in.

I slowly bring myself to a sitting position and then stand up. I must have drifted off sometime in the night, although I have no memory of it. And I must have slept very soundly, too, although I have no memory of dreaming, either. My right leg is aching. I must have slept on it much longer than I should have. I'm sure the discomfort will pass as the blood returns to my limbs. I put my body through quite a punishment yesterday and it's going to take a while to feel like my old self again.

I am suddenly aware of a strong sensation of thirst emanating from deep within my body. I'll be needing some kind of nourishment soon. I walk over to the shelves to see if I can find anything useful in the boxes they hold. I rummage through the boxes, blowing and wiping the dust off them as I go and kicking up a cloud of dust that hangs in the air, reflecting the rays of light hitting them from the tiny window.

As I rummage through the boxes, I do find some truly useful things...or they would have been useful if they worked. I find a flashlight with batteries that no longer hold a charge. It's the same for the small AM/FM radio I find. I find candles but nothing to light them with, an empty canteen, an empty packet of water purification tablets, and a small camping stove but no fuel to put in it.

It appears that whoever stored these items here was a prepper. The evidence is strong that this room was a place of refuge and survival for one or more persons at some point in the past. What happened to them, I can't say. I keep looking through the boxes, adding to the cloud of dust around me as I go.

I pull two identical, small unopened packages out of a box. "High calorie food bar," the label reads. "Five-year shelf life—4,800 calories." Jackpot! I quickly tear one of the packages open and hold its contents up to a ray of light to examine it. It appears to be in good condition and I don't see any sign of mold or decay.

I take a bite and the taste of rich chocolate overwhelms my senses. I savor each bite, chewing much longer than I should or even need to. I can't even remember the last time I've tasted chocolate and I'm not sure when I'll get to enjoy such a luxury again. It's a large food bar and my belly feels nice and full after finishing it. I'm sure I'll be needing every one of those calories to see me through the day—if I make it through the day. I put the other food bar in my pants pocket for later. I'll try to make the one I just ate do me for as long as I can stand.

I continue foraging through the boxes and I come to a box with an old mason jar and a small plastic bottle in it. I pick the Mason jar up and hold it up to the light. The fluid it contains is a dark-green opaque color…or maybe it's dark-gray. It's impossible to say for sure in the dim lighting. I twist the lid, hold it up to my nose, and inhale deeply. My body instantly recoils from the strong putrid smell that's burning my nostrils. I quickly put the lid back on the jar and secure it tightly. Whatever liquid the jar contains is now spoiled and I can't even imagine what it once was.

I put the jar with its foul contents back in the box and pick up the plastic bottle. It's heavy and it also appears to be holding a liquid of some kind. The bottle is not clear, so I can't visually inspect its contents. I take the lid off, very carefully bring it up to my nose—but not too close—and smell it. I don't smell anything. I stick my finger in the liquid and then taste it. Nothing…there's no taste that I can detect. I bring the bottle up to my lips and take a small sip. It's water! Oh, sweet water! I quickly gulp down all of the water and then return the now-empty bottle to the box from whence it came. My belly is now filled with life-giving nutrients and water. I couldn't have asked for anything more. I search through the remaining boxes but find nothing else I can use.

I turn my attention to the small table at the opposite end of the room. The table itself is nothing to look at…just a small metal utility table with folding legs. On it is a small record player attached to two small speakers. And on the record player is a record, a record that is covered in a thick layer of dust, like everything else in this room. I remove the record from the player and blow the dust off of it. I can barely make out the words "Motown Classics" in the faint light.

I put the record back in the player and then turn and walk away from it, and then I stop and turn back around. The record player is plugged into the wall. *No way,* I think. *It doesn't make any sense for electricity to be running to this forgotten place.* I slowly walk back over to the record player and a strong sense of curiosity washes over me. *Curiosity killed the cat*, I think and then pause in front of it. "But satisfaction brought it back," I say to myself.

I reach down to the old record player and flip the switch. The indicator light flickers on and the record starts spinning. Somehow I knew it would. I take the arm and place the needle at the beginning of the record and sounds of hissing and scratching fill the room. And then...music.

It's a sound that I haven't heard in years...real music. For a brief moment, I empty my mind of all cares and concerns and let the voice of the Motown crooner, whoever he is, fill the room. I don't even recognize the song the man is singing. It doesn't matter; it's beautiful. I close my eyes and take it all in from start to finish. I almost feel human again.

In what seems like the blink of an eye, the song ends. I could listen to that one song over and over again all day long but I know that such a thing isn't possible. I reach down and turn the record player off and watch the glow of the indicator light fade away, like the fading hope I have of making it out of this mess alive.

In the corner of my eye, I notice something at one end of the room that I have so far managed to completely miss. In such poor lighting, I could probably miss an elephant. I walk over to check it out and discover it's a curtain on a rod against the wall. Odd. I pull the curtain back, revealing a small alcove, a small room within the room. It's barely the size of a large walk-in closet. And then I see what I can only assume to be the former occupants of this little refuge, or what remains of them.

Sitting in a chair is the mostly skeletal remains of a man. I'm pretty sure it's a man because I can still see the facial hair attached to his mummified remains. In his arms is the skeletal remains of a small boy. At least I assume the child is a boy because of the way it's dressed. I walk into the alcove to get a closer look. There's a revolver on the floor underneath the man's skeletal arm, which hangs limply by his side. I see a large hole in the man's head and what appears to be a blood splattered stain on the wall beside him. The boy also has a large hole in his head and a large blood stain on the ground beneath his drooped head.

It's not hard to figure out what happened here. I can almost replay it in my mind. These two, probably father and son, sought refuge in this small room when Yellowstone erupted. They lived off their meager supplies for as long as they could. When it became clear that things weren't going to get better any time soon and their supplies were quickly running out, the man made a choice…a choice to end things before the real suffering started. It's a decision I'm sure countless others all around the world had to make, too. The man shot the boy first and then turned the gun on himself. It wasn't an act of cruelty but, rather, one of mercy.

I move a little closer to the man and the boy and then reach down and pick up the revolver. It's heavy and I can't tell much about it in the dim lighting. I slowly back out of the alcove and close the curtain behind me. I don't like disturbing the dead.

I take the revolver close to the small window where I can see it better. I don't know much about guns but the barrel is enormous. I look the revolver over thoroughly and see the word "Colt" stamped in one place. On the barrel it says "Python .357." It's a .357 revolver. I may not know much about guns but I know that a .357 is a very powerful and feared handgun.

I pull the lever holding the cylinder in place and it falls open. Two of the bullet casings are empty. It's no mystery where they went. I unload the empty casings, put the remaining four hollow point bullets back in the cylinder, and then snap it shut. Four shots. That's all I've got. I'll have to make them count. But with a hand cannon like this, four bullets could easily equal four kills, as long as they hit their targets. And the sentries. Even though I know I can't penetrate their torso armor with this gun with the hollow point bullets, I've got enough power in my hands to knock them down and make them think long and hard about pursuing me…maybe.

I take the overcoat hanging on the wall and put it on. Surprisingly, it's not a bad fit. I put the revolver in a large pocket on the inside of the coat but it doesn't fit. The barrel is too long. I tear a small hole in the pocket, a hole that's just big enough to let the barrel poke through on the inside of the coat. Perfect. I zip the inside pocket closed. I take the food bar in my pants pocket and put it in another pocket in the coat. I wrap the coat around me, button the front, and turn the collar up. It's cold outside and I won't be drawing any unwanted attention by wearing a coat. As long as I keep my head down, stay off the main roads, and don't do anything to draw attention to myself, I have a good chance of not being noticed.

But where do I go? Is there anywhere in this city that could possibly be safe from the manhunt that I'm sure is underway? Possibly. There's a chance I could find temporary refuge in some abandoned house somewhere or possibly in the community center where Dr. Bradshaw held his meeting yesterday. It could only be temporary because there's also the issue of finding fresh food and water. Since nearly all of the city's buildings were looted long ago, my chances of finding anything to eat or drink are slim. I got lucky today and I'm not so sure if such luck will repeat itself. I'm not sure if it's possible to make a life when all you have to rely on is luck. I can't help but fear that eventually I'm going to run out of luck.

My thoughts suddenly turn to Mom and Sarah and I am overwhelmed with a feeling of great concern for them. If there is a manhunt for me, it won't take the sentries long at all to find out where I live. The sentries will look for me there for sure. Mom and Sarah don't have any idea about what has happened to me, but that won't stop the sentries from questioning them. Will the sentries believe it when Mom and Sarah tell them they don't know anything about my whereabouts? I doubt it. I have a great fear that the sentries will do something truly nasty to them like torture them, or even kill them.

I have to reach them. I have to protect them. It isn't optional, and every additional minute that I waste here is another minute the sentries could use to hurt them. I would prefer to travel at night, but I don't feel like I have any choice. It's a risk I must take. It's time to leave this place.

CHAPTER 2

I OPEN THE DOOR TO MY little safe haven and am instantly greeted by a bright light that burns my eyes. I close them and lower my head to give my eyes time to adjust. I wouldn't exactly call it a sunny day, but it is a little brighter than usual. My eyes had grown accustomed to my dark sanctuary and I now need them to make a quick adjustment to my new surroundings.

I walk up the steps and then pause at the top. I turn around and take one last look at the small room that saved my life, and I think of the two occupants still inside. "Rest well, my friends," I say, and then turn and walk away.

As I walk down the road, I am suddenly aware of one undeniable fact: I have absolutely no idea where I am. In my haste to run away from my pursuer yesterday evening, I was only concerned with one thing: escape. I didn't care at all where I was escaping to, nor did I make any mental note of the path I took to get here. I'm lost, and before I can make my way to Mom and Sarah, I have to first figure out where I am. It's a big city.

This area is even more run-down than what I'm used to seeing, if that's even possible. I pass by an old house that was obviously involved in a fire of some sort. It's little more than a shell now, its beams long ago charred by a raging fire. I pass by a few commercial buildings, but they, too, look like they've seen much better days. They're old... probably built more than a century ago. I suspect they were nice places when they were new, but now they probably aren't even safe for the rats I'm sure inhabit them. And the road. It's a crumbling, patchwork mess of old asphalt, potholes, dirt, gravel, and weeds. Just great. It wasn't Yellowstone that did this. The lovely scene in front of me is the result of years of neglect.

I continue walking on this desolate road, looking for any building or landmark that looks familiar. I pass by a few people here and there, nothing to be too concerned with. I pass by one old woman on the side of the road begging for food in a small crowd of people. "I'm so hungry," she says to me as I pass by. I don't know why, but I stop and look at her. "I'll take anything you've got," she says. "I'm so hungry, my belly is aching."

I believe her. She looks severely emaciated, like pictures I remember seeing of concentration camp victims. I feel a strong sense of compassion for her and I reach into my coat for the food bar. I feel it in the pocket I put it in just moments ago. I start to pull it out, and then...

"Don't anyone make any sudden moves!" I hear behind me. I slowly—oh, so slowly—turn around and see two Detroit sentries approaching.

One of the sentries walks up to a man and grabs one of his arms. He uses his police baton to turn the man's face toward him. "No, not him," the sentry says.

The two sentries continue through the small crowd of people, looking each person carefully in the face. I'm afraid I know exactly who they are looking for. I take my hand off the food bar inside my coat, reach for the revolver, and slowly start to pull it out. My heart is beating fast. The fight or flight hormones are kicking in.

One of the sentries grabs another man and checks him out. "He's the one!" I hear the sentry say. The other sentry comes over, looks him over, and confirms he is the man they are looking for.

"You're late turning in your tribute," one of the sentries says.

"I tried, but I couldn't find anything! I tried so hard!" the man says in a desperate voice. His face is stricken with a look of horror. "Please give me another chance. I'll find two this week. I'll double my efforts. I'll—"

"You've had your chance," one of the sentries says. "You should have doubled your efforts last week."

"But sir, I'll—"

"Shut up! That's enough! It's time to face the consequences."

The sentry pushes the man hard in the chest, and the man falls to the ground. The sentry quickly stands over him and starts beating him hard with his police baton. The other sentry joins him and the two of them beat him mercilessly. They deliver hard blows to the man's stomach, head, his limbs, and his back. The man's face quickly turns into a bloody mess, and then he stops moving. In what seems like an instant, the sentries have beaten the life out of him.

It's best that way, I think. It's best for the recipient of such a terrible thing to get it over with before he even has time to think about it, unlike death on a cross where a person has hours or even days to think about what's happening to him.

"What are you looking at?" one of the sentries asks of no one in particular as he looks into the crowd. "All of you, move along."

I take my hand off the revolver, pull it out of the inside of my coat and continue walking. I then release the breath of air I was holding. I didn't even realize I was holding my breath. "Breathe, Adam," I say to myself. "In and out." My heart is still beating fast. Even though it's a cold day, I feel sweat dripping from my forehead. I walk away from the dead man behind me and don't look back. I can't.

I keep walking at a steady and deliberate pace, even though I still don't know where I am or where I'm going, and I keep my head down. I don't walk far down this poor excuse for a road until I see two more sentries in the distance talking with someone. I don't think they've seen me yet.

I duck into a recessed entrance to an old store of some kind and continue to watch them question different people. I see them go from person to person and occasionally see people shake their heads as though they don't know the answers to the questions they are being asked. But I think I know what they are looking for…or who. I am all but certain that I am the one they are looking for… the man who just yesterday ended the life of one of their comrades.

The two sentries start walking on the road in my direction. I have to hide somewhere, and fast. But where? I don't dare walk back out on the road. They would see me for sure. I feel trapped. I can see no place for me to go to except… inside.

I turn around and grab the doorknob of the door to the old store. It doesn't turn; it's locked. I look into one of the windows and see nothing but darkness. It's hard to see through them anyway since they are so dirty. Best I can tell, the place looks abandoned. I look around the corner of the recessed store entrance and see the sentries getting closer. I have to think of something fast.

I hear the sound of a latch turning on the door. Someone's inside and whoever that person is just unlocked the door for me. I don't have any choice. It's either go inside or face the sentries. I grab the doorknob again and turn it. It turns. I open the door and it makes a loud creaking sound as it moves. I quickly go inside, close the door behind me, lock it, and find a place to hide behind the front counter.

I watch from the safety of my hiding place as the two sentries come up to the door and try to open it, but the doorknob doesn't turn for them. It's locked. One of the sentries turns and starts to walk away while the other takes a good, long look through the window into the darkness inside. Every muscle in my body freezes as the sentry peers inside. I don't even dare take a breath. After what feels like an eternity, the sentry turns and walks away. My body relaxes and I allow myself to breathe again. I'm not sure how many more close calls I can handle.

I slowly stand up and look around. There are no lights illuminating this place. It's an old store of some kind and much of its stock is still in place, waiting for customers who will never come. And the windows…they are intact. This is unusual, and can only mean one thing: that someone has been protecting this place from looters. But who? Is it the person who unlocked the door for me? If so, where is he…or she? I can't say. Everything is as quiet as a mouse in here, and with the thick layer of dust that covers everything, nothing looks like it's been touched in ages. I can't say I feel safe in here, but I just might be safer here than out there.

I walk over to a shelf and examine its contents. It's filled with tubes of caulking. I see white caulking, clear caulking, and all manner of assorted brands. I walk over to another shelf. This one is filled with piping for plumbing, including various fittings, pipes, connectors, and other plumbing materials.

I slowly walk through a few aisles and check everything out. It seems I've stumbled into an old hardware store. It's filled with all manner of home repair and home improvement products…buckets of nails, cans of paint, stacks of flooring materials…it's all here. This place appears to be an old family-owned place, not one of those chain stores.

I walk over to the cash register. It's old. It looks like an old manual model. There's not a digital display, cord, or plug anywhere on it. I run my fingers over the keys and imagine the countless transactions it has made in its days. I punch the key that opens the cash drawer and it springs open. It doesn't contain any money but there is an old Timex watch in one of the bill trays. I pick it up and examine it. It's old and the wrist band is missing. The hands aren't moving, either. I wind the old mechanism a few turns and then watch as it starts ticking again. I might find some use for it later. I put the watch in my pants pocket and close the cash drawer.

I hear a faint sound somewhere in the back of the store, like someone just bumped into something, and I am instantly reminded that I am not alone here. I slowly reach into my coat and put my hand on the revolver's handle as I walk down one of the dark aisles. I start to take it out of my coat when I hear the unmistakable, loud sound of a pump action shotgun loading a shell behind me.

"Now you just hold it right there!" a woman's voice behind me says. "Don't you move, now, or I'll blow yer brains out!"

I freeze.

"Get yer hands where I can see 'em."

I slowly take my hand out of my coat and raise both hands in the air.

"Now turn 'round slowly so I can get a look at ya."

I slowly turn around. Before me, in the dim light, is a tiny, grizzled-looking old woman. She looks like she's barely five feet tall, and she's ancient. She's easily well into her nineties. She has wrinkles on top of her wrinkles, and I doubt that she even weighs ninety pounds. I suspect a strong breeze could carry her away, like a kite on a string on a blustery day. But still, she's at least strong enough to handle the shotgun she's holding. Old and grizzled as she is, I'll have to take her threats seriously. I'm sure she has enough strength in her bony fingers to pull the trigger on that street sweeper she's carrying and completely ruin my whole day.

"Now, slowly start walking toward me," the old woman says. "Let's get ya outta the dark so I can get a good look at ya."

I start walking toward her.

"That's enough; stop right there."

I stop.

She walks up to me and closely examines my face.

"You're a puny one, ain't ya?" she asks.

I say nothing back to her.

"Wait a minute," she says. "I know who you are. You're that guy who slit that sentry's throat, ain't ya? Ain't ya?"

I don't give her the satisfaction of a reply. I just keep my hands in the air and look straight ahead.

"Whatsa matter?" she asks. "Cat got yer tongue?"

"You've got the wrong guy," I say. "I'm just passing through."

"Yeah, I saw you duck in here and hide from them sentries. I may be old but I ain't blind. You are him, ain't ya?" The old woman walks a little closer to me and looks me over carefully. "You're famous now, didn't ya know? It's not every day that someone offs one of the king's troopers. Yep, word is spreadin' fast. Quite the hero, you are."

The old woman looks me up and then down and then shakes her head. "Can't see what all the fuss is about. You don't look like much to me. Too skinny for my tastes." She breaks out in raucous laughter, complete with a large, toothless grin.

I've got to get out of here. I look to the door to assess my options.

"You make a move and I'll fill your gut full of buckshot," the old woman says. "Alive or dead, it doesn't matter. You're worth the same to me either way. I prefer alive, but only because I don't want to clean up any messes today."

"Worth to you?" I ask. I'm not sure what she's talking about. Maybe she's just as delusional as she is old.

"Yep, you're valuable…worth your weight in gold, I'd say. You're worth a good —"

She pauses and looks me in the eye for a moment as she continues to point the shotgun at my belly. If that thing's loaded with buckshot as she says, she could easily cut me in half with it. I hope I don't get to find out.

"You really don't know, do you?" she asks.

"Know what?"

"Only that you're the first person to ever take out one of those sentries, is all. You're the first. You've caused quite a stir and people are talkin' about ya. Adam…isn't it?"

I don't reply.

"You gotta handsome price on yer head now, but ya didn't know that, did ya?"

I didn't. It wasn't even something I had considered, but it does make sense. If the sentries put a high price on my head, they know it'll be hard for me to find someone to turn to for help. It'll make capturing me much easier. And once they have me, they'll make an example out of me. I know they won't give me a quick death. No, they'll crucify me for sure.

"Don't you wanna know?" she asks.

"Know what?"

"What yer worth?"

I can't help but be curious. It's not like I've ever had a price on my head before. "How much?" I ask.

"Whoever turns you in doesn't have to turn in any more tributes for life.

"Not bad," I say, and it really isn't. I've never heard of anyone getting a lifetime free pass on the tributes. For something like that, I'd almost turn myself in; that is…if there was some way of knowing for sure that Mom and Sarah would be the recipients of the reward. But I can't exactly say that I trust the sentries to make good on any rewards or promises. Just the opposite, actually.

"Just think," the old woman says to herself. "A lifetime. Why, for a prize like you they might even let a person move inside the wall. 'Course, won't do me no good since I already got one foot in the grave. I'll let my grandson, Henry, turn you in. He's got a long life ahead of him. It'll be the best inheritance this ol' gal could possibly give him. Better'n this ol' place, anyhow."

The old woman walks over to a chair, takes it, and slides it in my direction. "What's the rush?" she asks. "Sit down. Stay awhile."

I slowly and cautiously sit down in the chair. It's hard and uncomfortable, but somehow I don't think my level of comfort is something she's even remotely worried about.

The old woman walks slowly behind me, keeping her shotgun trained on me the entire time.

"Now, don't you try anything," she says. I hear her doing something behind me but I can't tell what. "Don't wanna clean up no messes today."

I slowly start to reach for the revolver inside my coat. It may be the only hope I've got.

"I told you to…"

I feel a sharp sting in the back of my head, like when the sentry threw me into the brick wall yesterday. The world around me starts spinning out of control. Spinning, spinning…

CHAPTER 3

I OPEN MY EYES AND REALIZE the spinning has finally stopped, but the pain in the back of my head has not. It's throbbing. I try to say something, but for some reason my mouth doesn't want to cooperate. It just sounds like unintelligible garble, like someone moaning in desperation and pain. Even if I could manage to get a few words out, I'm not sure who I would be talking to.

Did I lose consciousness? I don't know. If so, how long was I out? Hard to say. I know only one thing: that I've got to find a way out of this mess before this evil granny either turns me in or does me in herself. Either way, I'm a dead man.

I look all around, but don't see the old woman. I try to stand, but can't move. Something's holding me down. I look down at my feet and see that they are tied to the chair I'm sitting in. I try to move my hands and instantly realize they are bound. I try to pull my hands and legs free from the bindings, but it's no use, they are tied tight. *The old biddy can tie a good knot*, I think to myself. *She's no Girl Scout, though, that's for sure.*

My gun. I no longer feel its weight in my coat. It's gone. I look around frantically and then I see it lying on a counter top nearby. If I could only get to it, I could…What? What could I do? I'm still tied up. I don't know. I don't have a plan but I've got to try to do something. Something is always better than nothing.

I place my feet firmly on the floor and try to scoot my chair. It scoots…but just a little, maybe a couple of inches. It's going to take a lot of scooting to get to my gun. I scoot a little bit more and then I hear her. I hear the faint sound of her footsteps approaching.

"Ah, I see you've come back around," the old woman says. "Gotta watch out for those things that go bump in the night, or in the daytime, in your case." She laughs.

The old woman comes closer, so close that her face is only inches from mine. I can smell her foul breath and rank body odor. She smells like a walking corpse.

"Oh, it's nothin' personal," she says. "It's just business, ya see…just business. Maybe if things were different, you and I might have become great friends. Yes, great friends. The two of us…pals."

The old woman walks over to the counter and picks up my revolver. She quickly spins around and holds it up to my head.

"Bang!" she says, and then laughs loudly. "And just where did ya pick up this fine piece, eh?" She looks the gun over carefully. "My, my," she says while she continues to admire the gun. "This truly is my lucky day. Even better than the ol' Pick Five Powerball. Couldn't spend all those millions these days if I had em'. Can't spend something that's worthless. I could wipe my ass with all those dollar bills, but I couldn't spend em'. But this," she says, still admiring the gun. "This is worth something."

"Why don't you just take the gun and let me go?" I say. "Keep it."

"And why would I do a thing like that?" she asks.

"Just my being here is going to draw a lot of unwanted attention from the sentries, even after you've turned me in. Do you think your grandson is going to turn me in, get a free pass on the tributes, and then that's the end of the story?"

"Something like that, yeah."

"That's not how it's going to go down. They're going to want to know how you got me, regardless of what you tell them. You're going to suddenly become very interesting to them. They'll keep a close watch on you from that point on, I guarantee it."

"Do say," she says, with a wild look on her face. "Do say."

"Tell you what," I say. "Let me go and you can avoid all of the unwanted attention. In exchange, I'll let you keep the gun. Like you said, it's worth something…a lot, actually. You can get quite a bit in trade with it. It's a good deal. It's a deal where we both win."

The old woman grins a wide, toothless grin, and then laughs loudly. "I have a counter-proposal," she says. Henry turns you in and I keep the gun. That way he and I both win…and you lose." She laughs again, even louder this time.

The old woman walks behind me. I can feel her tugging on the bindings holding my hands together. She walks back around and checks the bindings on my feet and then gets a look of satisfaction on her face.

"You're not going anywhere," she says. Henry will be here soon enough to take care of you. Then you'll be out of our hands."

I say nothing in return. This old woman is going to be a tough nut to crack. And if I can't strike some sort of bargain with her, then escape is my only option. But how? She won't let me out of her sight. And she's got me tied up so tight, my fingers are tingling from a lack of blood flowing to them. I've got to do something and do it fast, before this Henry person gets here. My window of opportunity is dwindling at a fast pace.

"Yep, Henry will be here soon," the old woman says again. "Now, I'm going to lie down until he gets here. Gotta get my beauty rest, ya know. Lookin' this good doesn't come easy once you get to a certain age." She laughs loudly.

I watch as she walks over to a small bed in a darkened corner of the room—a bed I didn't even notice before—and lies down. She places the .357 revolver on a small table beside the bed. I continue watching her closely for several minutes until the rise and fall of her chest as she breathes falls into the unmistakable rhythm of someone sleeping. And then I hear a soft snoring sound emanating from her body.

My window of opportunity just opened up in a big way. It's time to get to work.

CHAPTER 4

I LOOK FRANTICALLY AROUND the room for anything I can use to extract myself from this situation. This is an old hardware store, after all, so there's got to be something I can use lying on the shelves. Maybe this is the day I finally get to see a return on my investment from all those MacGyver reruns I used to watch so many years ago.

I would sometimes spend entire Saturdays sitting around the house watching MacGyver extract himself from one impossible situation after another. Naturally, Mom would tell me to go outside and get some fresh air, to enjoy the pretty day, and to not waste my time watching television. I would tell her that I might need to know how to do the things MacGyver does someday to get myself out of a tough spot. I was just joking, of course. I would keep on watching the show, ignoring both Mom and the pretty day outside. She would just roll her eyes and walk off, as if she knew it was a lost cause.

I don't know if I can "MacGyver" my way out of this mess, but I do regret not going outside and enjoying all of those beautiful days I wasted all those years ago. When a person is faced with his impending death at the hands of others, it makes him reflect on his life a bit and the things he should have and could have done differently. But of course it's too late now. Life doesn't give us any do-overs. The only thing we can really do anything about is what we've got in the present and in the future. If I'm going to have a future at all, I've got to make something happen right now. There's no time to waste.

I continue looking around the room for anything I can possibly use...an old box cutter, a saw blade, anything with a sharp edge on it. At this point, I'd even take a rusty old butter knife. Beggars can't be choosers. But as I scan the room I don't see anything I think would work. And besides, most of the store's stock is sitting on dimly-lit shelves, shelves that obviously haven't been touched in years and are covered in a thick layer of dust. I have no idea what most of them even contain. I try to pull at the bindings on my wrists but it's no use...they are tied tight and I fear any additional tension I put on them will only make them tighter.

As I look around a little more, it suddenly becomes apparent that the old woman is using this old store as her home. Near her bed, I see an old radio on a small table, a floor fan, a small bookcase filled with books, and a small desk. I wouldn't exactly call her accommodations comfortable, but she's got it better than many do.

The old woman continues to snore. As I watch her sleep, I can't help but think that she looks very much like a living, breathing corpse with her gaunt face and ancient wrinkled skin. I suspect she's not too far from such a fate. I continue looking around the room.

I turn my attention to a small pile of tools in a corner near me. They are lying just beyond a small metal filing cabinet. In the pile, I see an old hammer, a drill with no drill bit, a pair of pliers, and a screwdriver. I could possibly use one of them as a weapon if I could get to them…maybe.

The filing cabinet. It's old, like just about everything else in this room. It appears to have quite a bit of rust on it, too, including its corners. If I could make my way to the filing cabinet, there's a chance I might be able to use those corners to cut my bindings…if they are sharp enough. There's only one way to find out.

I start scooting my chair over to the metal filing cabinet. Inch by inch, I scoot along the floor, the dust on the floor softening the sound of my movement. I use my feet against the floor to pull the chair, no easy task considering my legs are tied to it, but somehow I make it work. When presented with a no-win situation, it can be truly remarkable what you can make happen, even when logic says it shouldn't or couldn't possibly work.

I continue scooting across the floor and then suddenly one of my scoots makes a loud screeching sound, like the sound of fingernails scraping across a chalkboard. I stop and look over at the old woman. She stops snoring at the loud sound and I see her smack her lips a few times, make a few strange sounds like she's talking in her sleep, and then she slowly but surely settles back into a relaxed sleep. I wait a few moments before I try moving again and then I hear it...that reassuring sound of snoring that says my captor is in another world.

I continue scooting along the dusty floor and make my way over to the rusty old filing cabinet. I position my chair so that my back is facing it. I stretch my bound wrist as far as I can and hold the rope that's holding my hands together against the filing cabinet's rusty corner. And then I start working the bindings against it as fast and hard as I can. I can no longer feel my hands. I can only assume they are purple from a lack of blood running to them. I've got to free them quickly.

I put more pressure against the bindings and feel one of the strands of rope snap. I continue working the ropes against the rusty filing cabinet corner when something catches my attention out of the corner of my eye. In my haste to free myself from my bonds, I almost didn't see it. Sitting on top of a counter top near me is the shotgun the old woman was wielding earlier. *Bingo!* I think. That shotgun just might be my ticket out of here if I can just free myself in time to get to it before Sleeping Beauty awakens or Henry the Horrible comes home.

I continue working on my bindings, working even faster and harder than before. The discovery of the shotgun has deepened my resolve and made me realize for the first time that I might actually have a chance of extracting myself from this mess. I feel another strand break, and then another. There can't be much left now. I pull hard on the remaining strands and then it happens… the remaining strands break and my arms fly free from their bonds.

I bring my hands around in front of me and look at them. They are purple, just as I suspected. I take a moment and loosen the remaining ropes around each wrist. As I do, I can see the color quickly return to them, along with a stinging sensation as life-giving blood fills them again. I then reach down to untie my feet. I don't even get so much as a chance to work on them when the old woman's snoring suddenly stops.

I sit back in the chair and look over at the old woman. She's starting to come around, all right. I see her stretch her arms, yawn, and then get up from her lying position and sit on the edge of her bed. She smacks her lips a few times and then sticks one of her fingers up her nose and starts picking. She then pulls her finger back out of her nose and examines the end of her finger closely. I then see her flick her finger, as though she's trying to flick whatever nugget she dug out of her crusty old nose away from her. She belches loudly and stands up and scratches her butt.

The old woman grabs the revolver off the little table beside her bed and walks over to me. Her back is so twisted and hunched over from her advanced age, I'm surprised she can even walk. Somehow, she manages. I quickly put my hands behind my back as if I'm still bound. If she decides to check my bindings again, it's all over for me. I doubt I'll get another chance to make an escape.

"Oh, were you trying to get to this?" she asks as she pats the shotgun on the counter top. It's clear that I'm not sitting in my original position. I don't care for her to know I've scooted around, as long as she doesn't know my hands are free.

The old woman picks up the shotgun and presses the end of the barrel against the side of my head. I hear a loud click and can feel the vibration of the trigger being pulled. My eyes close hard and my body jerks spontaneously in reaction. And then…nothing. I'm still alive. I open my eyes and take a deep breath.

"It's empty," she says as she puts the shotgun back down on the counter top. "Haven't had any shells for it in ages. It's harmless enough. Looks scary though, doesn't it?" She laughs and then pauses and looks at me as though she's waiting for some kind of response.

I say nothing and stare blankly at her. I feel a sinking feeling in the pit of my stomach, as though the hope I had a moment ago of freeing myself and getting out of here suddenly vanished with the revelation that the shotgun I was trying to get to is now useless.

"Well, it was scary enough to fool you," the old woman says and then cackles. "Henry should be home soon enough and then he can turn you in. Yes, this will all be over soon enough for you. But first, a little tea for me."

The old woman walks over to an area of the store I can't see, and I hear the sound of water pouring and some other sounds I can't quite make out. I assume she's heating water in a kettle of some kind.

With the old woman out of sight, I reach down and try frantically to undo the bindings holding my feet, but I don't make any progress. The knots she has tied are very tight. It's going to take awhile to undo them, time I'm not sure I have.

I hear the old woman's footsteps walking in my direction and I quickly return to my previous position with my hands behind my back. She comes close to me and brings her face close to mine again.

"Oh, it's going to be fun when they get hold of you," she says. "They won't give you a quick death, that's for sure. Oh, no. Not after what you did. No siree. They'll torture you awhile. Beat you, they will. They're going to make you feel sorry for what you did before they do you in."

I say nothing to her and try to look away from her gaze.

"Being the first to take out a sentry kind of makes you a celebrity," the old woman says. "Hot damn! I gotta celebrity in my house! Can I get your autograph? Oh, wait…I guess you can't since you're a bit tied up at the moment." She laughs loudly.

I am not amused by her attempt at humor, or mockery, or whatever it is she's trying to do to me.

I hear the whistling sound of a boiling kettle from somewhere on the other side of the room and the old woman goes over to it.

"Tea time," she says as she walks away from me. "Gotta have my tea. Good for your health, ya know."

I hear the old woman pouring hot water and then the sound of someone knocking loudly on the front door diverts my attention.

"Ah," the old woman says. "Henry's home…"

CHAPTER 5

THE OLD WOMAN WALKS over to the door, unlocks it, and opens it. I hear the sound of heavy footsteps walk in. Where I'm sitting, I can't see this Henry person. The counter blocks my view.

"Do you want some tea, Henry?" the old woman asks.

"Nah, you know I don't drink that stuff," he says.

"It's good for ya. It'll put hair on your chest."

"But I already have hair on my—"

"Never mind that. Did you get anything today?"

"Nothin'"

"Well, I did."

"What're you talking about?"

"Come. Look and see."

I hear two sets of footsteps walking toward me. The old woman comes into view first and then a burly man in his mid-twenties appears. He's tall, maybe six feet, I think. He looks like he hasn't shaved in weeks and his dark hair is long and unkempt, like most people's these days. He appears to be surprised to see me and looks me over carefully.

"What have you done, Gran? Who is this man?" Henry asks.

"You don't recognize him?" the old woman asks.

"Should I?"

"Well, let's just say he's famous."

"I don't know, Gran. Why's he all tied up? Did he try to hurt you or something?"

"Let me give you a hint. There's a price on his head."

Henry doesn't say anything. He just stares at me blankly with his mouth open.

"This man is going to buy your freedom," the old woman says. "You don't recognize this wanted man?"

Henry closes his mouth, swallows, and then continues breathing out of his mouth again. He reaches a hand up inside his shirt and scratches something. And then his eyes slowly widen.

"This isn't the guy who killed that sentry, is it?" Henry asks.

"In the flesh!" the old woman says, with a look of deep satisfaction.

Henry walks over to me and looks me over.

"You sure it's him? Henry asks. "Ain't much to him."

"It's him," the old woman says. "Caught him runnin' from the sentries."

Henry gets closer to me as he continues to look me over.

"You're kinda famous, ya know. People been talkin' 'bout you."

"So I hear," I say flatly.

Henry walks back over to the old woman. They both continue to stare at me, like two vultures standing over their prey.

"You gonna turn him in and get the reward, Gran?" Henry asks.

"No, shit for brains," the old woman says. I ain't gonna turn him in. You are. It won't do me any good to turn him in at my age. Just think…no more tributes for the rest of your life."

Henry stares blankly at the wall beside me with his mouth agape. "No more tributes," he repeats. "Ever. You did catch something today! You reeled in a big one!"

"What did I tell ya?" the old woman says and then takes a sip of tea. "This old girl's still got it. This calls for a celebration! I'm gonna fix something extra special for your dinner. While I'm cooking, you're gonna go report the good news. When you come back with some sentries to escort our friend away, it'll be ready."

Henry's open mouth turns into a smile and his eyes widen. "You're already makin' me hungry, Gran," he says.

"Now go," the old woman says. "Don't waste any time."

Henry turns and lumbers around the counter separating me from the door. The old woman walks behind him. He pauses in front of the door and turns to the old woman. "You sure we got the right guy?" he asks.

"He's the one. Now, get going."

Henry leaves, and the old woman locks the door behind him. She then walks back over to me and stands right in front of me. She takes another sip of tea.

"Are you getting a cramp from sitting there?" she asks and then laughs.

"I'm fine," I say calmly.

"Well, you won't be fine for long."

The old woman takes another sip of tea and stares straight into my eyes. "I got some cookin' to do. Now don't you run off anywhere and miss all the fun." She walks away from me to the area of the room I can't see where she prepared her tea a few minutes ago. I hear her shuffling around, and the sound of pots and pans and utensils clanging and other cooking sounds fills the room.

I reach back around and start working on the bindings holding my feet again. I know I don't have much time and every second counts. I pull and tug at the ropes, but the knots holding them are tight. I look all around me for anything I could use to help pry or cut the ropes. And then I see the pile of tools I noticed earlier just on the other side of the metal filing cabinet. The screwdriver. That might do the job. It's a flat-head screwdriver, but it might just be sharp enough to tear through my ropes if I use enough force. And I think I can reach it, too, but it won't be easy.

I slowly and carefully stand up with my feet still bound to the chair. I crouch down in front of me and stretch my arm toward the pile of tools. I can almost reach it…just a little more. I stretch my arm out a little further and finally grab the screwdriver. I quickly return to my chair and sit down. I don't dare risk getting caught standing up. I lean down and start picking the knot with the end of the screwdriver. A few strands break. Encouraged, I work even harder to free myself. A few more strands break and then…I stop.

I have a sudden revelation. *Of course!* I think. *Why didn't I think of that earlier?* This screwdriver might just help me out in another way. But I need to get that crusty old woman back over here first. I put my hands back behind my back, concealing the screwdriver with them. *Here goes nothing*, I think.

"Bring me some of that tea, you old biddy!" I yell across the room.

I hear a loud crash as the old woman drops a pan or maybe a pot on the floor. "What the…" she says in a startled voice.

I hear the sound of her feet moving quickly across the floor and then I see her. The amused expression she previously had as she mocked me is now gone. In its place is one of rage and anger. She walks up to me but doesn't get too close.

"I may be old, but I ain't deaf," she says. "Did you just give me an order?"

"You heard me; damn right I did! Now bring me some tea, woman. I'm thirsty."

"Oh, you're thirsty," she says with a look of indignation. "Well, let me tell you something."

She moves a little closer to me.

"You just wait until…"

A little closer.

"When Henry gets here with those sentries, they'll—"

I quickly swing my arm around and with every last ounce of strength I can muster, I drive the screwdriver hard into the side of the woman's head. The entire length of the screwdriver's blade sinks into her skull and blood sprays onto the floor in front of me and drips down my hand. I watch as the life force fades from her, and then she falls forward, straight into my lap. I quickly push her limp body off of me and she falls on her back on the floor, the screwdriver still stuck in the side of her head, and her now lifeless body staring at the ceiling above.

She's dead.

I take a deep breath and lean back in the chair. "Old biddy had one foot in the grave anyway," I say to myself. I watch as a pool of blood quickly grows underneath her head.

There's no time to celebrate. I'm not out of this mess yet. I don't know how long it will take for Henry to find a pair of sentries and return. I stand, and then crouch down and grab the screwdriver imbedded in the old woman's head. "I'll be needing that," I say to her corpse as I pull the screwdriver out of her. Blood pours out of the open wound onto the floor.

There's no time to wipe the blood off of the screwdriver. I sit back down and immediately go to work picking the knot again. I continue working where I previously left off and in just a moment I have one leg free. I start working on the other leg. Just as before, the strands slowly but surely break as I pick at them with the blade of the screwdriver. As the last few strands are about to give, I hear voices just outside the store. Someone's coming!

I pull hard with my leg with everything in me against those last few strands and they finally break. I'm free! I get up and quickly run across the room to where the old woman was cooking earlier. The windows are so dirty and the room is so dark, I doubt whoever is just outside could see me. There must be another way out.

I hear a loud knocking on the door followed by the sound of someone trying to turn the doorknob. I can only assume it's Henry with a pair of sentries. I look everywhere for a door and don't see one, but I do see a window. I open the window, climb up, and put one leg out. I swing around to put my other leg out and then I remember…the .357. I'll be needing it.

I climb down from the open window and run back into the room where the old woman was napping earlier. I hear a key turning in the door and see the knob turning. There it is! The .357 is lying just where she left it on the small table. I grab it and run just as the door opens.

"Gran?" I hear in the other room. "We're back."

"Check the room," I hear a different man's voice say.

I hold the revolver close to my chest, dive headfirst through the open window, and land with a hard, graceless thud on the concrete below, right next to some broken glass. There's no time to count my blessings. I quickly jump up and start running down the side alley I've found myself in. At the end of the alley I take a side road, and then another side road until I come to an area with several abandoned cars. I try to open the back door of one car with tinted windows. It opens with a loud squeaking sound. I get in, shut the door, and lock it.

The interior stinks of mildew and the cloth seats are ripped and torn. The radio is missing. The floorboard is covered in what looks like a layer of thick mold, but none of this matters. The only thing that matters is that I've found a place to hide until the sentries Henry found get tired of looking for me and return to their regular patrol. I slide my body down into the seat, take a deep breath, and slowly release it.

For the next few hours, I'll call this place home.

CHAPTER 6

THE PASSAGE OF TIME CAN accomplish many things. Given enough time, the body can heal itself of many illnesses and injuries. Many conflicts and feuds have been completely forgotten as the years ticked by. After a few years, some even have a hard time remembering what all the fuss was about. Some grow wiser as they age while others just grow older. And for the sentries of Detroit, a few hours could mean all the difference between being involved in a manhunt and becoming bored and distracted when the manhunt results in false leads and dead ends. That's what I'm hoping for... counting on, actually. I'm betting everything that the sentries that were mere seconds away from catching me just a few short hours ago have now become distracted or bored and are no longer looking for me in this area.

I open the door of the old car that has been my home for the past few hours. I'm glad to finally get a little fresh air. After several hours of breathing the moldy, stale air of the car's closed interior, sitting downwind of a trash dump would be refreshing in comparison.

I slowly step out of the car and look all around me. I see nothing. Of course, that's no guarantee that there are no sentries around, but the chances of them lurking in the area of this old side road are not very high. I pull my coat around my body and button it. I flip the collar up around my neck and start walking away from where I came earlier. I have no idea where I am or where I'm going. Hopefully, I can find a landmark soon and get my bearings.

I pass by a man begging on the side of the road.

"Help a poor old man out?" he asks with an outstretched arm holding a cup.

It's not unusual to see beggars on the streets, but this man catches my attention for something he's wearing...something I want. His clothes are ordinary enough but on his head is an old, worn fedora. Worn with my overcoat, it would be a great help in concealing my identity. I approach the old man.

"I'll take anything you've got," he says.

It suddenly occurs to me that I have nothing to give him. I put my hands in my pants pockets and feel something in my right hand, something I picked up earlier but had completely forgotten about. I pull the old Timex wristwatch out of my pocket and look at it. It's still ticking away.

"How about a little trade, my friend?" I ask.

"A trade?"

"A working watch for your hat." I extend my open hand to him with the watch in it.

"It works?"

"See for yourself." The man leans forward and squints hard, as though he is having trouble seeing.

"So it does," he says. "So it does. Haven't seen one of those in awhile."

"So, what do you say? The watch for your hat."

The man studies the simple watch carefully and then looks up at me.

"Done."

He smiles and takes the watch from my hand. He then takes the hat off and hands it to me. I take it and put it on. It's a little loose on my head, but it'll serve my purposes nicely.

"Good trade," the man says as he turns the watch over and over in his hands, examining it. "Good trade."

"Much obliged, my friend," I say and then walk off.

I tip the front of the hat to conceal my eyes, put my hands in my overcoat pockets and start walking. Where I'm walking to is not in question. I had plenty of time to think about it during my time hiding in the car. I've got to go home and check on Mom and Sarah, to let them know I'm okay, and to let them know that I'll have to go away for awhile. No, where I'm going is not in question, but finding my way there is. I've got to reach Mom and Sarah before the sentries do, if they haven't already. I fear for their safety and I am overcome with an overwhelming feeling of guilt for the unwanted attention they are sure to receive, if they haven't already.

I continue walking.

CHAPTER 7

I DON'T HAVE TO WALK FAR before I run into a familiar landmark, and then another. I regain my bearings quickly and walk home on the back roads and back alleys, always keeping my head down as I go. I don't encounter any crowds on the way or see any sign of the sentries harassing anyone. Oddly, it's an uneventful trip.

I'm almost home and I'm excited to finally get to see Mom and Sarah again, to tell them all that has happened to me, to scratch Juno's ears again, and even to have her lick my face. I'm just glad to be back after everything I've been through.

I can only imagine what Mom must be thinking. She's a worrier, so I'm sure she's worn a path in the floor from pacing back and forth in anticipation and concern. She'll probably run up to me and embrace me in a long hug. I can already see the tears running down her cheeks. And Sarah. She'll try to act like it's no big deal that I've been gone for so long, but she'll break down and give me a hug when she's certain Mom isn't looking.

I'm sure they will both have at least a million questions for me.

I walk up to the door, turn the knob, and walk in. Mom is sitting in a chair sewing something. Sarah is sitting in a corner of the room reading a book of some kind. Neither of them look up.

"Hi guys," I say. "Wait till you hear what happened to—"

"Close the door, Adam," Mom says. She quickly returns her attention to whatever it is she's sewing.

I close the door.

"Watcha reading, sis?" I say to Sarah.

"Adam, would you care to stoke the fire?" Sarah asks. "It's cold in here."

"Yes, Adam. It's cold," Mom says. "You let some of the heat out when you opened the door."

"Uh, sure," I say. It must be at least eighty degrees in here. I can already feel beads of sweat forming on my brow.

I walk over to the wood burning stove and open the door. I take the fire poker and turn a few pieces of burning wood over. As I'm stoking the fire, I look over at Mom. I see her look up at me and for a moment our eyes meet. She quickly looks back down at her sewing. She has a strained, concerned look on her face. Much more strained and concerned than usual, that is. I stoke the fire some more and then look over at Sarah. She glances up at me and then quickly returns her gaze to whatever it is she's reading. Strange.

Something's wrong here…very wrong. The tension in the room is thick. I slowly look around the room but see nothing unusual. Not that I'd see a sentry if there was one here. I set the fire poker off to the side and close the stove door. I slowly stand up and start walking toward my bedroom. *Don't make any sudden movements*, I think to myself.

I walk into my bedroom and close the door behind me. I look around the room but see nothing amiss. Everything looks just as I left it.

"Juno?" I say quietly. "You in here, girl?"

I hear a faint whimpering sound coming from beneath my bed. I walk over to it, kneel down, and look underneath. The room is dark and it's even darker underneath the bed but I can barely make out a dog's paw. And then I see the reflection of her eyes in the dark.

"What are you doing under there?" I ask. "Come on outta there. Come on."

Juno slowly moves her body toward me, but I can sense fear in her, like she wants to come to me but she doesn't want to come out of her hiding place. She's still whimpering. I've never seen her act like this before. I pull the covers back and call to her again.

"Come on Juno. It's just me. What's got you spooked?"

Juno comes a little closer...just close enough to stick her snout out from underneath the bed. I extend my hand to her and she licks it.

I take hold of her and slowly pull her out from underneath the bed.

"There. That wasn't so bad now, was it?"

Juno moves quickly away from me and cowers in a corner, shivering. She tucks her tail between her legs and continues to whimper. I walk over to her and scratch her ears some more.

"What is it, Juno? What do you see?"

I look around the room again but see nothing. I hear nothing. But I'm afraid I know exactly what Juno has seen and heard. Is she still seeing it? I don't know. But she may still be smelling it. The powerful canine sense of smell is legendary.

I hear the sound of water hitting the floor in front of me and look down at Juno again. She's peeing on the floor. Her shivering and whimpering are getting stronger. There's no question about it at this point. There are unwelcomed guests in the house, sentries... somewhere, although I don't think they are in this room. I've got to get out of here quickly.

I walk over to the window and look out at Detroit and the wall that surrounds it off in the distance. It's still there. I slowly open the window, being careful not to make any noise. A blast of cool air blows into the warm room. I actually welcome it, considering how hot it is in here.

I hear a knock at the door. I don't dare answer it. I don't think it's Mom. She usually knocks and then asks if she can come in. Sarah doesn't even give me that much courtesy. She usually just barges right in. I hear no voice on the other side of the door. No, there's someone else knocking. It's not Mom or Sarah and I have no intentions of sticking around long enough to find out who it is.

There's another knock at the door. This one is louder, more forceful.

I quickly jump up on the open window sill, put both of my legs through it, and drop to the other side. I slowly close the window behind me. Just as it closes I see the door open.

I run.

CHAPTER 8

I RUN AWAY FROM MY own home with the simultaneous feelings of both relief and fear. I am relieved to escape whatever was waiting for me. I have no idea why they didn't reveal themselves before I had a chance to flee, but I'm sure there was a reason.

Perhaps the sentries found a way to sneak into the house without revealing themselves to Mom and Sarah. That would explain their bizarre behavior. If Mom and Sarah sensed a presence in the house, it would explain why they were acting the way they were…as though nothing was wrong and my walking through the door after being gone overnight was a normal event. It would also explain why they cut me off mid-sentence when I tried to explain to them what happened to me and where I'd been. They were trying to protect me from revealing anything.

But I am also leaving home with a great deal of fear. Not for me, but for Mom and Sarah. I have no idea what the sentries will do to them. They could reveal themselves and make their lives a living hell, or they could stay concealed and leave just as quietly as they arrived. I have no way of knowing. I do know that Mom and Sarah are both tough and street smart. I've seen both of them extract themselves from some truly hairy situations before. As much as I want to go back and protect them, I know it isn't an option. It can't be. Just my being there puts them at risk. No, I can't go back. I would be a much greater help to them at this point if I just stayed away. And so it shall be.

I pull my hat down over my eyes and flip my coat collar up around my neck to conceal my identity as best I can. I start walking along the open road in front of me. I walk past old buildings, old abandoned cars, around potholes, and on the opposite side of the road from beggars. I'm not walking toward any specific destination. I only know that I'm walking away…away from the city. I've got to get as far away from the city as I possibly can, as far away from the sentries as I can. It may be my only chance at survival. I don't know if I'll ever see Mom and Sarah again if I do leave the city, but I don't have any choice. I can't see any alternative.

I haven't been away from the city since before the eruption of Yellowstone and I have no idea of what to expect. I don't know what's waiting for me. It could be a little of everything…or nothing at all. Perhaps my mind is playing tricks on me and I'm imagining the worst. All I need is a simple place to sleep, a source of clean water, and some kind of sustenance. I'm a simple man with simple needs. Surely I can find what I need.

I keep walking away from the city. The minutes turn into hours and the further away from the city I go, the smaller the buildings get, and the further apart they are spaced. Things are looking less urban as the hours and the miles both tick by. I pass by the occasional skeletal remains of some poor old soul who didn't make it as I walk. Some of them are right in the road, while I see others off in the distance in the fields, parking lots, in the ditches, and in other areas. Apparently, cleaning up the old remains hasn't been much of a priority for whoever still lives out here, if anyone does.

Come to think of it, I'm really not sure if anyone does live this far out. I've traveled several miles since I've seen anyone. Of course I've heard rumors and stories of the wild people who still inhabit these places, but I'm not sure if they are true. I'm not sure if things are any safer out here than they are back in the city. I suspect it's just as dangerous, but in different ways.

Out here there's absolutely nothing stopping a person from robbing you, beating you, or even killing you. There's no law to speak of here. I suspect it's a lot like the old Wild West, except without all of the horses, gunslingers, saloons, and other such trappings. If there's anyone left out here, that is, and I'm not entirely sure there is. At least, I haven't encountered anyone out here…yet.

I've been walking for hours and I'm now very tired…and hungry…and thirsty. My feet are hurting, too. I see a small stream in a wooded area and walk over to it. It looks clean enough. I hang my hat on a tree, kneel down in front of the stream and scoop a small amount of water up in my cupped hands. I bring it up to my nose and smell it. Nothing. That doesn't necessarily mean it's clean, of course, but it's a good sign. I take a small sip. It tastes cool, clean, and oh, so refreshing. I drink all of the water in my hand and then go for another scoop, and then another, and another until my thirst is satisfied. Now, about my need for something solid…

I look around the wooded area on both sides of the stream for anything I can eat and it doesn't take long at all to find some wild greens. Edible wild greens are all around us. Most people just have no clue which plants they can eat and which ones they can't. A lifetime of going to the grocery store will condition a person that the forests, meadows, streams, and valleys have nothing to offer. It just isn't so.

Years ago when Mom, Sarah, and I were learning how to eat off of the land while we were making preparations for some unknown future disaster, we used to have contests to see who could find the most wild plants to eat. We would all find so many different edible plants in no time at all. We would then make huge salads out of them and feast on our bounty. I don't care about feasting today. I just need enough to give my body a little nourishment. I take a few minutes and eat a variety of wild greens until I feel satisfied. I retrieve my hat from the tree I hung it on earlier, return to the road, and continue walking.

It's nearly dark and I need to find a place to bed down for the night. I don't need much. Just basic shelter is all, just a place to stay dry from any rain…and from any wild animals that might find me interesting. I see a small house up ahead that looks abandoned and start walking to it. It's a quaint little bungalow, nothing special. I walk up to the porch and see that one of the windows is smashed. It's already been looted. I actually prefer it that way. If I stay here, this place shouldn't attract any attention from looters or anyone else. There's essentially nothing here of interest to anyone except a guy like me. Perfect.

I walk up to the porch and wipe what looks like several years of dust off of an old chair and sit down. I take my hat off and place it on a small table beside the chair. I sit back, take a deep breath, and slowly let it out. It feels good to finally give my tired feet a rest. I hear a faint buzzing sound off in the distance. It's probably just a swarm of insects of some kind.

As I take a few minutes to relax in the chair and watch what little bit of remaining daylight there is fade away into the night, I think about what it would be like to bring Mom and Sarah to a place like this and live out here away from the harassment of the sentries. And why not? So far, it seems peaceful enough. We could find an old abandoned home and fix it up a bit. The water seems to be drinkable and we could continue hunting for fresh meat and gathering wild edible plants. Essentially, our lives really wouldn't be all that different from what we currently have, except we wouldn't have to deal with the daily harassment from the sentries. The more I think about it, the more I like the idea. How bad could things really be out here when compared to dealing with the sentries?

The buzzing sound is growing louder. Whatever type of insect swarm it is, it sounds like it's heading in my direction. I suppose it's time to go inside and find a place to bunk down for the night. Just a clear spot on the floor will do nicely. I grab my hat, put it back on, get up and walk over to the door. I turn the doorknob and the door opens. The buzzing sound is even louder now. It sounds like it's almost upon me, and it no longer sounds like a swarm of insects. It almost sounds like something mechanical.

I close the door and walk down from the porch to investigate. The sound is very loud now, like it's just above me, but I still don't see anything in the dim twilight. And then I see it…but just barely, because it's so small. It almost looks like a child's toy, like a small radio controlled aircraft of some sort with its four small rotors holding it up in the air like a small helicopter.

A drone!

That was the buzzing sound I heard. I've got to get away from it. I start to turn and run toward the house when…

Flash!

A bright flash of light explodes above me from the drone's body. It just took my picture and it probably just relayed the image to its sentry handlers in the city. It won't take them long to identify me and send a team to track me down. But that doesn't mean it will be an easy task for them. It's a big area out here. If I can get away from the drone, I've got a decent shot at evading them.

I start running away from the house. I don't make it far before I trip on something and fall to the ground. My hat flies off my head and I frantically feel around on the ground for it, but I'm unable to locate it. The sudden flash has temporarily blinded me. It's almost dark now and everywhere I look I see nothing but the flash of light that was seared into my retinas. It'll fade in a few minutes, I'm sure, but for now I am struggling to see where I'm going.

I pick myself up off the ground and continue running but the loud buzzing sound of the drone's rotors follows right behind me. It's not going to give me an easy escape, that's for sure.

"Don't move!" A loud voice emanating from the drone says. I ignore it and continue running just as fast as my feet will carry me.

"You can't outrun it," the voice behind me says. "Stop running now and your life will be spared."

I can't even remember the last time the sentries spared anyone's life. It's a ruse; I'm sure of it. I keep running. My eyes are slowly adjusting and the world around me is coming back into focus. I see a wooded area just ahead. It would be difficult for the drone to fly through it. I start running toward it when I feel two sharp pains in my upper back, like two angry hornets just stung me. And then it hits me.

At first I don't feel pain, only paralysis. I have no control of my body and I fall to the ground in front of me. And then a wave of incredible, intense pain surges through my body. I can't breathe. The drone has shot me with some sort of electroshock gun and I'm suddenly on the receiving end of thousands of volts of electricity. The muscles in my arms and legs contract uncontrollably as I ride the lightning and writhe on the ground.

And then it stops.

I take in a deep breath and slowly bring myself to a sitting position on the ground. All of the muscles in my body are aching. I reach behind me and pull the wires out of my back. Pulling them out hurts just as bad as it did when they went in. I continue holding the wires in my hand as I stand up. The buzzing sound…it's still there… just above me.

Flash!

Another bright flash goes off above me; again it throws my vision off and I can't see the world around me. I've got to get away from this thing, and fast. The forest. I think it's just ahead of me. If I can just get to it, I can…

"This is your second warning. There will not be a third," I hear from the drone just above me in a deep, loud voice.

The wires. I'm still holding them. It suddenly occurs to me that they are attached to the drone. I take the wires and start pulling the small drone closer to me, like reeling in a large fish. But it's no easy task. The pull from the drone's rotors is surprisingly strong. And the wires. I am sure they are cutting into the flesh in my hands as I pull, but I don't have any choice.

The drone finally comes within reach and I reach out and grab hold of its small body, letting go of the wires as I do. I have it but my grip on it is not firm. I can feel my hands slipping, no doubt from the blood in my palms from pulling so hard on the wires.

I take the small drone and smash it on the ground. Over and over I pick it up and slam it hard on the ground. I pick up a small rock I find from feeling around on the ground and continue to pummel my little nemesis. I hear cracking sounds coming from the object in front of me, no doubt the sounds of pieces of little machinery breaking. I reach down and feel wires spilling out of the drone's broken body and yank them loose for good measure.

Confident that my mechanical pursuer is now destroyed, I lie back down in this field I'm in and stare up into the dark, cloud-covered sky above me. I slowly let my eyes adjust to my surroundings. My racing heart slows and my breathing is no longer labored, but my body is aching all over. My hands are bleeding and I'm pretty sure my back is bleeding, too, where the wires from the drone's electroshock gun dug in to deliver their shock.

I know I have to get up and get away from this field. I can't lie here for long. It's almost a certainty that another drone or even a swarm of drones has already been dispatched to finish the job the first one failed to do. It's only a question of how long it will take them to get here. I have no way of knowing. I slowly prop my beaten body up on my elbows and then force myself to stand. I see the wooded area not far in the distance. I start walking toward it and then…

I hear music.

I hear some sort of song that I don't recognize coming from somewhere off in the distance, just over a knoll in the large field in front of the house I just came from. Strange. Where there's music there's got to be someone behind it, or several people. Maybe they're having a celebration of some kind. Maybe they can help me. Maybe.

I start walking in the direction of the music. This may or may not be a good idea but I have no way of knowing for sure unless I check it out. I slowly make my way across the field and over the knoll. As much as I'd like to, I simply can't make my body move any faster.

As I come to the other side of the knoll, I see a light not far in the distance. It's faint, like that of a small lantern or maybe a flashlight near a lone tree in the field. I start walking to it. Whatever the light is, it also appears to be the source of the music as well. The closer I get to the light, the louder the music becomes. I get almost right up to it before I can make out what it is.

The light is a flashlight with a red wand attached to the end of it, like the police used to use to direct traffic. It's standing upright on the ground with a few small rocks around its base to support it. And the source of the music is apparent as well. Right beside of the flashlight is a small, battery-powered radio and cassette player. It's old and from the looks of it, it's seen many years of hard use. I still don't recognize the song that's playing. It's some kind of country song and the woman who's singing it is going on and on about losing her man to another woman. Well, cry me a river. I never did like country music anyway. I'm more of a rock and roll guy myself. That would explain why I didn't recognize the song.

I reach down and turn the radio off. No use polluting my ears with that stuff if I'm the only one listening to it. I pick up the flashlight and check it out. It's nothing special, but I can certainly put it to use.

Wait a minute. It suddenly occurs to me that there has to be someone else out here if there's music playing. But why would—

"Now!" I hear someone say from somewhere nearby. My feet are suddenly pulled out from under me and my body is swept up into the sky.

And then it all becomes very clear to me. The radio. The flashlight. It's no different than putting a piece of cheese on a mousetrap. Those things were the bait and I'm the mouse. Only this mouse was dumb enough to fall for it. And now I'm caught in some sort of trap. Will whoever set the trap let me go as long as I promise not to come back in his house or will he feed me to his house cat? I'll know my fate soon enough.

CHAPTER 9

MY BODY IS BEING HELD in the air by some kind of large piece of fabric, like a bunch of coffee beans in a burlap sack. My first thought is that it might be an old parachute recycled into some kind of man trap. And the leaves. My body is completely surrounded in a dense layer of leaves. They must have been used to conceal the fabric while it was lying and waiting on the ground for its next victim. I try to feel my way to freedom, try to crawl out of this large sack that now holds me, but it's no use. I see a faint glow on occasion in the leaves as I move around, no doubt the flashlight that lured me here.

"Okay, let it down," I hear from somewhere below me. "Let it down slowly."

I feel the sudden sensation of movement, like I'm descending down to the earth below. I have no idea how high up I am in the air. I try to feel around again for a way out.

"No use squirmin'," I hear again below me. "You ain't goin' nowhere."

I stop moving. As much as I hate to admit it, the phantom voice is probably right. It'll take awhile to untangle myself from this mess, and time is a luxury I don't have right now. May as well save my energy. I suddenly feel the sensation of terra firma on my body. I'm finally on the ground, but I'm still very much wrapped up. I remain still and can feel the folds of cloth being pulled away from me one by one.

"Don't you move now, you hear?"

I say nothing.

"Are you sure it's not an animal, Daddy?" a second voice says. It sounds like the voice of a young girl.

"Ain't no animal, Magpie," the man says. "It's a woman."

"How do you know, Daddy?" the girl's voice asks. "Does she have long hair?"

"No, short."

"Maybe it's a man."

"Nah. Too skinny to be a man."

The last piece of fabric is pulled away from me and I am now exposed in the pile of leaves that I'm lying in. Before I even have a chance to see my captors, a bright beam of light hits me right in the eyes. I recoil from it and hold my hands up over my face to get a reprieve from the blinding light.

"Well, whad'ya know?" the man says. "It *is* a man."

"Ain't got much meat on his bones," the girl says in a tone of voice that sounds like she's disappointed.

"That's okay. We can still make a stew out of him."

"As long as I still get his liver."

"Of course, Magpie. I know that's your favorite part. I'll fry it up real nice for ya."

And just like that I now know what my fate is going to be: I'm to be slaughtered and cooked for dinner, no different than a cow, deer, or some other animal. Maybe they'll even save the leftovers and make Adam sandwiches out of me the next day. Fantastic.

"Now don't you try to be no hero now, you hear me?" the man says.

"I hear you," I say. "I hear you."

The man lowers the flashlight to the ground in front of me and my eyes slowly come into focus. Before me is a man with long unkempt hair, a full beard, and he's wearing a pair of the thickest glasses I think I've ever seen. He's dressed in camouflage military fatigues and a camouflage boonie hat, and he's pointing what looks like an AK47 rifle at me.

By his side is a young girl; at least I think she's a young girl. She has a strong wild look to her, like she's been raised by wolves, which may not be too far from the truth. Her long, frayed red hair doesn't look like it's seen a brush in ages. Her face is covered in dirt and freckles, and she's wearing dirty jeans and an old torn shirt. I'm guessing she's six or maybe seven years old. A life of hardship is probably the only life she has any memory of. Nevertheless, I'm having a hard time feeling any sympathy for someone who is determined to eat my liver.

"I want you to slowly stand up," the man says. "Nice and easy like."

I stand up…slowly.

"Nice and easy," the man says again as he slowly walks toward me. "I'll spill your guts right here if I have to. You won't be the first by a long shot."

I say nothing. I have no reason to doubt him. I suspect he's already taken many lives. The man shoves the barrel of the AK47 into my ribs.

"Nice and easy," he says again, like some kind of broken record.

The man runs his hands over my body, frisking me for any kind of concealed weapon. He runs his hand over the .357 tucked away inside my jacket and stops.

"What've we got here?" he asks.

He reaches inside my coat and slowly pulls the revolver out.

"Now I suppose you're going to tell me this is for huntin' squirrels and such?" he asks.

"It's for protection," I say.

"Uh-huh." He takes the revolver and places it in a large pocket on his camouflage jacket. "Well, you won't be needing it anymore."

He continues to frisk me and places his hand on my hunting knife. He slowly pulls it out of its sheath. "And I suppose this is for skinnin' all those squirrels."

"Something like that."

"Right," he says and hands the knife to the girl. "I need you to hold on to this." The girl takes the knife and holds it firmly with both hands. "Now be careful," he says to her.

He turns his attention back to me.

"Now, here's what we're going to do," he says. "You're going to turn around and start walking and I'm going to follow right behind you. If you try anything, I shoot you. Got it?"

"Got it," I say. I turn around slowly.

"Now start walking."

I start walking, but where I'm walking to I don't know.

"What are you going to do to me?" I ask. I'm fairly certain I know the answer but for some reason I ask anyway.

"Do to you?" the man asks. "Why, you're our guest…our dinner guest. We're all gonna have dinner together."

That's what I was afraid of. I swallow hard and keep walking…and look for any opportunity I can find to extract myself from this situation.

CHAPTER 10

I CONTINUE WALKING STRAIGHT ahead, and the man and girl follow close behind. I hear them walking behind me and I don't dare try to make a run for it. I'm sure the man has his rifle pointed at my back. One simple pull of the trigger would be all it would take to end my life.

We come to the main road.

"Now make a left turn on the road and keep walking," the man says.

I do as he says. I don't know how long we walk, but it's now completely dark outside. The sky is overcast like it usually is, and there is no moon or stars shining down on us, nor are there any streetlights. It's so dark I can barely see the ground in front of me.

"Right here," the man says. "Take the path to your right." I look to the side of the road but only see a thickly wooded area. I see nothing that looks like a path.

"Go on, now," the man says.

I walk to the side of the road…and then I see it: a very narrow path cutting through the dense forest growth. It's nearly invisible to anyone who wouldn't know what to look for and I have no idea how the man even saw it, as dark as it is.

I start walking on the narrow path. It's not an easy path to traverse and I'm having to constantly push branches and other brush out of my way just to move forward. Occasionally, I trip on some unseen branch, rock, or something else on the ground. I have no idea how my captors behind me are faring on this challenging path, nor do I care.

After several minutes of hiking, we come to an area that opens up in front of me. Before me is a small shack with a dim light emanating from within. I suspect this is a place the man built deep in the woods to protect him and the girl from others. It's a safe house. As I get closer to the shack, I detect a foul smell…the smell of something rotting. And then, as I get a little closer, I see it: human remains lying in the yard. It's little more than a skull attached to a spinal column. A cold chill surges through my body at the gruesome sight in front of me and it becomes readily apparent that if I don't find a way to escape, that will be my fate as well.

"I told you this morning to drag that off and bury it somewhere," the man says. "If you leave trash out in the open like that, it'll attract bugs."

"But you put it there!" the girl says.

"Don't you sass me, girl! If your momma was here right now, she'd take you and —"

"I wish mommy *was* here!" the girl says and then starts crying uncontrollably. "Mommy! Mommy! I miss you so much!" she wails.

The man walks over, kneels down in front of the girl and puts his arms around her. "I'm sorry, Magpie. I shouldn't have said that. You're my girl and I love you." He holds the girl tight against his body and she stops crying.

"It's okay, Daddy," the girl says.

"No, it's not okay. I'm gonna do better. I promise. Look, we've got each other, a safe place to stay, and plenty to eat. We're doing real good, a lot better'n most these days."

"I know," the girl says.

The man quickly gets up and turns his attention back to me.

"You just keep walkin' now," he says to me. "Maggie, get the door."

The young girl runs past me, unlocks the door, opens it and runs inside.

"Inside," the man says behind me.

I slowly walk inside the small dwelling. The simple room I walk into is dimly lit by an oil lamp on a small table. There's not much to see: an old chair, a bundle of blankets in one corner, a few pots and pans in another corner. The shack is shoddily constructed. It appears to have been made from whatever materials the man could carry here by hand. There may not be much to it, but it's a safe haven in a crazy world for the two people who live here. It's their home. I pause at the main entrance to take it all in.

"Keep walking," the man says.

I keep walking straight ahead and come to the entrance to a small kitchen area. In a corner of the small kitchen, a well-fed calico cat is eating something out of a bowl. It looks up to me with wild eyes and hisses loudly.

"Keep walking," the man says again.

I walk straight through the small kitchen until I come to another door.

"Open it," the man says.

I turn the doorknob and push the door open.

"Walk," he says.

I walk through the door and into some sort of enclosed back yard, if you can call it that. There is no grass, only bare ground with a few small weeds growing in areas. And the entire area is enclosed by a chain link fence topped with a coil of razor wire. With the exception of the razor wire, the area looks almost like it was built as a place for a dog to run around in. In one corner of the yard, I see what looks like a large dog cage.

"Walk on over to the cage," the man says.

I walk over to it.

"Get in," he says.

I kneel down on the ground and crawl in head first. The man closes the cage door behind me and places a large padlock on it. The cage stinks of feces and urine. The smell is so strong that my body retches for a few minutes, like it's trying to throw up, but nothing ever comes up. After a few minutes, I start to get used to it and I'm finally able to breathe without retching.

The cage is much smaller than I first thought, and I am having trouble moving around in it. After a few minutes of struggle, I manage to find a comfortable position…as comfortable as I can possibly get, considering the circumstances. I look around for the man but don't see him. The back door to the house I went through to get here is closed. He must have gone back inside while I was busy retching and trying to hold in my lunch.

I look around to see if there's anything I could possibly use to help me, but don't see anything of consequence. I grab hold of the cage door and push hard on it. It's no use. It's a sturdy metal cage designed to contain a large dog…or a weak, emaciated man. It's all just a matter of perspective, I guess. I lean back in my cage and try to save my energy. I may need all of it I can muster the next time the man returns. Gun or no gun, I fear I'm going to have to confront him if I'm going to have any chance of getting out of this alive.

A span of time passes as I sit in my cage thinking of every possible escape scenario, none of which are any good. I am jarred out of my thoughts by the sudden sound of the opening of the back door to the shack. I look up and see the little girl walk out with the calico cat following right behind her.

The girl walks up to my cage and stares at me blankly. She doesn't even blink. She's holding a doll of some sort. I can tell that it was an expensive doll when it was new, not one of those cheap ones you buy at the local big box store. It's wearing an ornate but very dirty dress. Its long hair is a frayed mess, not unlike the girl holding it. And one of its eyes is hanging by a thread out of its socket. It was a fine doll in its day, but now it's only a sad reflection of the world all around it. The calico cat jumps on top of my cage and lies down.

The girl continues to stare at me with a blank expression. So I stare back. Our staring contest continues for what feels like several minutes until I can't take it anymore.

"What?" I ask flatly.

"I'm Maggie," she says.

"So I've gathered."

"And this is Carrie Anne," she says, holding the doll out in front of her.

"Lovely," I say.

I hear a rustling sound above me and look up to see the calico cat staring down at me. It hisses loudly at me.

"What? You, too?" I say to my feline tormentor.

"His name is Mittens," Maggie says.

"Well, Mittens is just charming," I say. The cat hisses loudly again and sticks one of its paws through the cage above me as though it's trying to get to me. "Just a barrel of fun to be around."

The girl doesn't reply but instead just stares at me again, as though she's contemplating something.

"I'm going to eat your liver," the girl says in a matter-of-fact tone, as though she were simply telling me I have a cowlick in my hair or that I have some food stuck in my teeth.

"Why would you do something like that?" I ask.

"Because it's my favorite!" she says. "Daddy always saves it for me."

"I see."

There's a low rumble of thunder above me and I can both feel and hear rain drops start coming down all around me. The cat jumps off the cage and runs in the house through the still-open door.

"Come back inside, Maggie," I hear from the door. I look up and see the man calling out to the girl. "Remember what I said about playing with your food."

"Well, I gotta go," Maggie says. "See ya tomorrow."

"Yep, tomorrow," I say without even so much as an ounce of enthusiasm.

The girl runs back in the house and closes the door behind her. The rain is now coming down harder. I lean back in my cage as the heavy raindrops hit me and soak into my clothes. It's dark and I was already cold, and now with the heavy rain, my body is going to get even colder... much colder.

I try imagining myself walking on a warm beach in the summertime with the sun beating down on me and my feet sinking into the warm sand with every step I take. Mind over matter. It isn't working. I'm still cold and one of my legs just contorted in a painful cramp.

It's going to be a long night.

CHAPTER 11

THE SUN IS SLOWLY COMING up and I hear a rooster crowing somewhere far off in the distance. It's morning. I made it through the night but I'm not in good shape. The rain stopped sometime during the night but my clothes are soaked, and I'm cold. I'm so cold that my body is shivering uncontrollably.

I look around frantically for anything I could use to help me, but I don't see anything. I grab the cage door with both hands and rattle it furiously, but it doesn't budge. As the night turns into day, I can see my surroundings much more clearly now. The padlock holding the cage door closed is large and strong. The metal the cage is made from is very thick. This cage could easily contain the biggest, baddest dog in the neighborhood.

The door to the shack suddenly opens and the calico cat runs out, followed by the man holding the AK47. He walks over to me.

"Sleep well?" he asks.

"No. As a matter of fact, I didn't," I say while trying to gain some control over my shivering body.

The man unlocks the large padlock, takes it off, and then opens the cage door.

"Get out," he says. "Slowly."

I slowly crawl out of the cage feet first.

"Stand up," he says as he points the rifle at me.

I slowly turn my body over and get up on my knees, and then slowly bring my body to a standing position. I pull my coat tightly around my body but I'm not sure if it's helping or hurting since it's completely soaked. The man points with the end of his rifle toward a door in the fence I hadn't noticed before.

"Walk," he says.

I start walking toward the door. I stop in front of it and the man comes around in front of me and removes another large padlock. He opens the door and then nods toward it.

"Let's go," he says.

I walk toward the now open door and hesitate as I'm about to walk through it. I have a very good idea about what's about to happen. He's going to take me somewhere away from the house and kill me, like an animal being taken to be slaughtered. He's doing it early in the morning so it'll be done before the girl even wakes up. And then I'm sure I'll be butchered and turned into a meal.

"Keep moving," the man says.

I walk slowly through the door. No use in getting in any hurry. It leads to a narrow path in a wooded area, not unlike the one we took to get to this place yesterday. I start walking on the muddy path into the woods. It's slick from the rain we got last night and I slip and slide in several places and even fall down once. The man walking behind me doesn't fare much better.

After several minutes of walking on the muddy trail, we come to a small, moss-covered rock outcropping. I walk out onto the outcropping.

"Stop here," the man says.

I stop. I look all around but see no way of escaping. I take in a deep breath and then release it. *At least it's a peaceful place to leave this world*, I think.

"Down on your knees," the man says.

I slowly get down on my knees, first one knee and then the next. *He's probably going to shoot me in the back of the head*, I think. *Make it quick!* I take another deep breath and hold it and then I close my eyes. The longest seconds of my life tick by as I wait for the end to come. And then … it doesn't.

I hear the man walk away from me. I release the breath I was holding and open my eyes to see what's going on. I see the man place the rifle against a rock. He then pulls a large knife out from inside his coat and starts walking back toward me.

Of course, I think. *Can't waste a bullet on me. Ammo is much too hard to come by.*

The man takes a few steps toward me with a look of determination in his eyes, eyes that are covered by incredibly thick glasses, but he doesn't get far. He takes a few steps and then loses his footing on the slick, moss-covered rocks underneath him. In an instant, his feet fly out from under him. He lands hard on his side and his head bounces off a rock, creating a large gash in his temple, and slinging his glasses from his head. The knife he was holding flies from his hands and lands on the ground between him and me. Blood is now pouring from his wound.

In an instant, time freezes. The man looks up at me, or looks in my general direction, I should say. I suspect he can't see a thing without his glasses. The blood that is pouring off his temple is getting into his eyes. I look at the man and then down at the knife on the ground in front of me, and then I go for it.

I lurch from my position kneeling on the ground toward the knife and land just in front of it. The man also moves frantically to get the knife he just lost, but he isn't quick enough. I reach it just before he does, grab it, and then jump on top of the man and try to lunge the knife into his chest. Just as I'm about to sink the knife into him, he grabs my arm and pushes hard on it to push it away from him.

Blood is pouring profusely from his head now and the moss-covered ground beneath him is becoming crimson stained. Like two deer with locked horns in a fight to the death, the man and I are in a battle that will lead to one of us dying. I'm pushing the knife down as hard as I can while he's pushing my arm away from him as hard as he can. I see fear in his eyes, just as I suspect he sees hope in mine. And he's growing weak. The more blood he loses, the more his strength fades. And I'm growing stronger. As I feel his strength diminish, my resolve increases.

I quickly move my hand that was holding the man down from his shoulder to his neck and squeeze as hard as I can. He begins to make gurgling sounds, as though he's struggling to either take a breath, swallow, or both. His entire body heaves and his eyes bulge out as his body reacts to being cut off from life-giving air.

I continue to squeeze the man's throat just as hard as I can. His face is now turning a dark shade of crimson. It matches the crimson that is flowing from his head. He is still making gurgling sounds and saliva is now dripping from one corner of his mouth.

The man looks as though he's about to pass out. Reflexively, he takes the hand holding my arm that is keeping me from stabbing him away and reaches up to his throat. With my arm now free, I force the knife hard into his chest with every last bit of strength I've got. His entire body clenches, as though a large surge of electricity just shot through it, and then it goes limp.

My captor is dead.

I release the man's throat and look into his now dead eyes that stare blankly into the sky. This man was going to make a meal out of me. How many others has he killed and eaten? How many lives has he snuffed out for his own satisfaction?

I feel rage build inside of me and I let out a loud guttural cry of frustration into the forest around me. I continue to cry out and tears are now flowing down my cheeks. I feel so much anger toward this man, this man who was about to kill me for food, but it's not just that. I feel so much frustration over this situation I'm now in. I am angry at the sentries, at King Darius, at not being able to take care of my family, at not being able to have a life. I am angry at the world around me, and at myself. Above all, I'm angry at all of the senseless killing.

I begin stabbing the man in the chest. Over and over again, I stab his lifeless body while crying and wailing. My blade sinks into his flesh and blood pours out of the slab of meat that just a moment ago was alive.

I stop my outburst of crying, wailing, and stabbing. It was cathartic, and the rage that was in me is no longer there. I roll away from the dead man's body, lie on my back, and stare into the cloud-covered sky above. I hear birds singing and flitting about in the trees above and around me. Oh, to be as free as a bird, to not have a care in the world. How nice it must be!

CHAPTER 12

I LIE BESIDE MY DEAD CAPTOR and stare into the sky for several minutes as my body recuperates from what it just went through. A fight to the death tends to take a lot out of a person, at least it does me.

Feeling somewhat better, I slowly bring myself to a sitting position, and then stand up. It's quite a scene. The man's body is covered in blood. His face, his hair, and his body are all soaked. It's also all over the ground. A large pool of blood has formed under the man's body, but it has also splattered onto the rock outcropping around me from my stabbing spree. It's on my clothes, too, but thankfully the coat I'm wearing is dark. I'm sure it's on my face and in my hair. My hands are covered as well.

I pick up the knife I just stabbed the man with and clean it. I unstrap and remove the knife sheath off of the man's body, strap it to my waist, and put the knife in the sheath. It's not my trusted old hunting knife, but it'll do just the same.

I could leave the body here and let the vultures take care of it, but I'm afraid the little girl will find it. She's already seen more crazy things in her short existence than most people see in a lifetime. No use in adding to her emotional scarring.

I grab the man's body by his ankles and start dragging him into the woods. Maybe if I drag him far enough from this place, the girl won't find him. Unless she smells him, that is, which is a possibility. I drag him as far as I can, which isn't very far. I don't want to waste too much valuable energy on him. I don't want to spend any time digging a grave for him, either. I gather handfuls of leaves and pile them on his body until he is sufficiently covered. It's not much of a burial, but I know I'm treating his body with far more respect and courtesy than he would have afforded me. At least it will keep the buzzards off him.

I leave the man in the woods and return to the rock outcropping. The AK47 rifle the man was carrying earlier is in the same place he left it, leaning against a rock. I pick it up, release the magazine, and it falls to the ground. I pick it up and examine it. It's fully loaded. I put it back on the rifle and then drape the rifle across my back with its sling.

I walk back to the shack on the narrow path I took to get here earlier. It's still muddy from the heavy rain last night. I try to be careful on the path but I can't help slipping and sliding in places as I go.

I make it back to the shack and walk through the open gate in the fence I went through earlier when I was certain I was walking to my death. I close it behind me. Not that it matters; it just feels good to know that I just closed a door to something I don't want to remember. If only it was as easy to close the door on the memory and never have to think about it again or see it in my dreams. If only it was so easy, but it never is.

I walk into the shack through the back door and start searching the premises for anything I can use. I look through drawers and cabinets in the small kitchen area. Nothing.

"Daddy?" I hear from the next room over. I stop looking in the kitchen. There's nothing I can use here anyway. I walk to the tiny living room and see Maggie sitting on the floor playing with her doll. She looks up at me with a look of surprise on her face.

"Where's Daddy?" she asks. Her eyes are wide and she looks both terrified and confused at the same time. I'm sure she thought I was her dad rummaging through the kitchen a moment ago.

"Daddy's gone," I say.

"When's he coming back?" she asks.

"He's not coming back." I look through the room for anything I can use while talking to her, but it's no use. The room is sparse; there's almost nothing in it.

"Did you do something to Daddy?" she asks.

"You ask too many questions," I say as I walk to the small bedroom. I see the .357 revolver and my hunting knife and sheath lying on a small night stand. I pick the revolver up and put it back in my inside coat pocket. I strap my hunting knife back to my leg and leave the knife I just took off the man's dead body on the small table. I find nothing else in the room I can use.

"But he was just here a little while ago," the girl says.

"Hush now!" I say back to her.

"What did you do to—"

"Shut up, Maggie!" I yell.

The girl starts crying loudly and huge tears are now falling down her cheeks. There's no point in sticking around any longer. There's nothing else here I can use. I'm just thankful to be leaving this place with my life. I walk out the front door and slam it hard behind me.

I see a small storage shed near the edge of the yard. It was very dark when I was first brought to this place. The small building was easy to miss. I walk over to it. It's shoddily constructed, like the shack. I open the unlocked door and immediately see an old motorcycle, but little else. There are a few old tools on a bench, a storage bin with potatoes in it, a small gasoline can, and a small stack of magazines on a high shelf that's almost out of reach.

I'm hungry. The food bar I found earlier is still in one of my coat pockets, but I'd like to save it for when I can't find any food, if possible. I sort through the box of potatoes but none of them look like anything I want to eat. They've been here for awhile. Most of them feel soft and mushy, like they are rotting, and nearly all of them are sprouting roots. No thanks; I'll pass. I'm hungry but I'm not *that* hungry. It can wait. I toss one of the potatoes I was examining back in the bin and turn my attention to the magazines.

I stretch my arm and reach up high and pull one of the magazines down. I look at the cover and instantly I understand why it was placed out of reach. "Late Night Fantasies," the cover says. Below the title is a scantily clad woman in a provocative pose. A porno rag. *Why, you dirty old man,* I think. At least he had enough consideration to keep it out of the little girl's reach. I don't open it. I place the magazine back where I found it and then turn my attention to the motorcycle.

It's a Triumph, a brand of motorcycle that was very common in the United Kingdom, but never really caught on in the United States. I can't help but wonder how it ended up in this tiny shack. It's clearly old, too, maybe a 60's model. These old bikes with their single-cylinder engines didn't have much power, but at this point I really don't care. As long as it runs, that's all that really matters.

I roll the bike outside to have a better look at it. It's in rough condition. It has dings and dents all over it and the paint is faded and chipped. The tires are dry-rotted and cracked from age. They are also covered with mud. There's very little dust on the bike. These are all good signs that indicate it's a bike that is used regularly.

I open the gas tank and look in. It's difficult to see in the tank since it's overcast, but it looks like it's almost empty. I go back in the storage shed and grab the small gas tank. It's light, but I do hear a distinct sloshing sound as I pick it up. At least there's something in it. I open the can and smell its contents. It's definitely gasoline. I put the funnel lid back on the small can, take it over to the bike, and empty its contents in the bike's tank. It may not be much, but at least it'll get me a few miles down the road, and a few miles away from this crazy place. I'll take it.

With the tank now filled with as much fuel as I can find, I sit on the old Triumph and get ready to fire it up. I squeeze the clutch, put it in neutral, and then…I realize I don't have the key. It may be old, but it still has an electrical system. The empty keyhole on the bike's console is a dead giveaway.

I dismount the bike and look in the storage shed again for the key. I look in every nook and cranny, even underneath the magazines. Nothing. It must be in the house.

I walk back in the house but don't see the girl anywhere, nor do I hear her. It's quiet…almost too quiet. I pause for a moment and think. *If this were my home, where would I keep the key to my only source of transportation?* The bedroom. It's the only thing that makes any sense. That's where I'd keep my motorcycle key, anyway.

I walk back into the tiny bedroom I searched just a few moments ago and look through it again. Not that there's much to look through…some bedding on the floor, a small nightstand, a few other personal effects. Again, I turn up empty-handed. On a hunch, I reach up under the nightstand and feel around for anything that might feel like a key. Nothing. I open the nightstand drawer and feel around inside of it. Bingo! I find it attached to a hook on the inside of the drawer. *Not bad*, I think. *It fooled me the first time around.*

Time to get out of here. I walk out of the bedroom back into the tiny living area. No sooner do I set foot in it when I hear a blood-curdling scream and see the girl running toward me from the kitchen area with a large knife in her hand. She runs right up to me and tries to stab my thigh, but I catch the knife she's wielding mid-swing. I grab her other arm, too. She's animated and is screaming and wriggling hard to get free.

"Where's my daddy?" she yells loudly. "What did you do to my daddy?"

I continue to wrestle with my pint-sized assailant. She drops the knife. I pick her up and hold her tightly against my body. It's not a hug. I'm certainly not feeling any love for her at the moment. Rather, it's a restraint. I hold her arms down by her side as she continues to wail and cry uncontrollably.

Minutes pass and once she realizes I'm not letting her go until she calms down, she finally stops struggling. Her wailing slowly turns into a heavy cry, a light cry, and then her tear factory runs dry. She's no longer crying or struggling. She's limp in my arms. I carry her into the bedroom and place her on the bedding in the floor. She immediately curls into a fetal position, buries her face in the covers, and doesn't make a sound.

I feel no sympathy for the girl. How can I? I turn and walk out of the little shack and return to the motorcycle. I have no idea what will become of the girl, nor do I care. She looks more like a wild animal than a girl anyway. This is where she belongs...out in the wild.

I straddle the motorcycle once again, insert the key, and turn it to the on position. The indicator light on the tiny dash lights up. I squeeze the clutch with my left hand and then press the start button. Instantly, the single-cylinder engine roars to life. I put it in first gear, slowly pull out, and head out on the trail I first took to get here yesterday evening.

I turn around and take one last look at this place where I almost lost my life. The little girl is standing in the open doorway watching me leave. She has an anguished look on her face. It's a look of intense confusion and fear. I see no tears on her face. No time to get sentimental over a girl who was going to turn me into a meal. I continue down the narrow path and concentrate on reaching the main road.

It's a difficult path to traverse and my tires occasionally slip in the mud. I dodge branches and brush as I slowly ride along the path. Occasionally, a branch I didn't see smacks my body and I nearly lose control of the bike.

After several minutes of traversing the narrow path, I finally make it to the main road. I take it and start riding back toward the city. I have no idea what I'm going to do when I get there or how I'm going to survive, but somehow I have a feeling that I might fare better there than out here in this wild place. At least I know the city. I'm familiar with it. I at least have a chance of finding a place to hide until things blow over and the sentries completely forget I even exist. I don't know how long that will take…weeks, maybe months, but I don't have any choice.

I continue riding toward the city. I don't travel far…maybe two or three miles before I see her face in my mind. I see the little girl's face on the porch as I pulled out and rode away. I see the anguish on her face; I can feel it. I try not to think about it and concentrate on trying to think of a good place to hide out once I return to the city, but it's no use. Every time I get her face out of my head, it returns. I see her tears; I hear her cries in my head.

I stop the bike in the middle of the road and the Triumph's engine slows to a gentle idle. I know she won't last long if I leave her behind. She'll starve to death, most likely. I turn the bike around and face the direction I just came from. *Do I really want to do this?* I ask myself. No, I don't, but I know I'll never be able to live with myself if I just leave her behind. She may be one step away from being fully wild, but she's somebody's child…or she was. And besides, if I leave her to die, am I really any better than her father, the man who fully intended to kill me, cook me, and eat me? No, I'm not. I won't let myself sink to such a level of depravity.

I don't know how much gas I have left, but it can't be much. No matter. I pull out and start riding back to the shack and to the little girl…to Maggie.

CHAPTER 13

I ALMOST MISS THE TURNOFF to the path leading to the shack. It's very easy to miss. I can see why the man chose that location for his home. It's very cleverly concealed. I have to give credit where it's due.

I ride along the narrow path again, dodging branches and bushes as I go. Once again, the path opens up to the small yard and I see Maggie standing in the open doorway looking out. She's heard me approaching, no doubt. She's holding that raggedy-looking doll, Carrie Anne, in her arms.

I pull up to the shack, turn the bike off, lean it on its kickstand, and climb off. Maggie's face still looks anguished. She looks like she's trying to cry but I don't see any tears. Her body is shaking. She may be a child but she fully understands the gravity of the situation.

I slowly walk up to her and slowly, gently reach out and take her by the shoulders.

"I'm truly sorry about your dad," I say. "I'm so sorry about everything." And I am. They aren't just words. At this moment, I wish with everything in me that I could take all of this away from her, that I could somehow give her a normal life. At her young age, she shouldn't have a care in the world. She should only be concerned with getting good grades in school, with making friends, and enjoying and exploring the world around her. Her life is a twisted mess and I wish so much that I could fix everything, but I know I can't. I don't know if she'll ever have anything even remotely close to what I would call normal. What's done is done.

Maggie tries to say something, but I can't make it out. Between her shaking body and her sniffles, the words she's trying to say don't make any sense.

"Listen, Maggie," I say. "I can't leave you here all by yourself. You won't make it if I do. Do you understand me?" She nods her head to indicate she does. "I'm going to take you with me. I don't know how but I'm going to take care of you."

Maggie doesn't say anything. She looks into my eyes and continues sniffling and shaking. I reach out with both arms and bring her close to my body. I hug her tightly, although she doesn't return my hug. Her arms hang limply by her side. For several minutes, I feel her body shaking in my arms and I can hear her sniffles. And then, she stops shaking. I continue to hold her tight to me. As I do, it occurs to me that this may be the first hug this child has ever had. Another minute passes and then something I didn't expect happens…she wraps her arms tightly around me.

I continue to hold her for several minutes and then we slowly release our embrace. I take her by the shoulders again and she looks straight into my eyes.

"We're going to make it," I say to her. She nods her head up and down.

"Are you hungry?" I ask. She nods her head up and down again.

I reach into my coat and pull out the food bar I was saving and hand it to her. She takes it and then just looks at it as though she's never seen a candy bar, protein bar, or any other food item in a plastic wrapper. I doubt that she has. She starts turning the food bar over and over in her hands, examining it. It's obvious that she doesn't know what to do with it.

"Let me show you," I say. I extend an open hand to her and she hands the food bar to me. I open it, completely remove the plastic wrapper, and hand it back to her.

"Go ahead," I say. "Take a bite."

Maggie takes a small, cautious bite of the food bar and starts chewing. In an instant the expression on her face changes from one of fear and sadness to one of wonder, excitement, new discovery, and joy. Her eyes grow large and I detect a bit of a smile. Yes, she's definitely smiling.

She takes another bite, a much bigger bite, and chews fast and hard.

"Careful," I say. "Don't take too big of a bite." She grins and continues chewing.

"Mmmmm," she says.

"Good, isn't it?"

"Yeah!"

I watch her finish the entire food bar and then she rubs her belly with a sly grin on her face. It's a look of satisfaction.

"We can't stay here, Maggie. We have to leave," I say.

"Why can't we stay here?" she asks.

"Because there's no food here...I mean good food, like the kind you just ate. Also, it's not entirely safe here, either."

"Where are we going to go to?

"Away from here...back to the city."

"Well, can Carrie Anne come, too?"

"Of course she can. She can ride on the motorcycle with us."

"Okay," she says. "Let's go."

I walk back to the motorcycle and Maggie follows, holding her doll. I take the AK47 rifle that was slung across my back off and place it on the ground. I know it could prove valuable later on and I hate to give it up, but there's no way Maggie can ride behind me while I'm carrying it. I get on the motorcycle and help Maggie climb up behind me.

"Hang on tight to me," I say. I feel her small arms wrap around my waist and squeeze tight. I look down and see Carrie Anne in one of her hands.

Once again, I ride on the narrow path that first brought me here and onto the main road. I aim the little Triumph toward the city and start riding. I don't know what I'm riding to or what fate awaits me when I get there. I only know that between here and there, the city is the lesser of two evils.

CHAPTER 14

IT'S LATE IN THE EVENING and what little daylight that is penetrating the ominous layer of dark clouds above is quickly disappearing. I can see the Detroit skyline off in the distance. I was worried the small amount of gas in the tank wouldn't get me very far, but thankfully, it has. That's one advantage of riding a bike with only one cylinder…great gas mileage.

I continue riding toward the city and my surroundings are becoming increasingly more urban. The buildings are now closer together and I'm starting to see a few people here and there. I know that I'm going to have to ditch the bike soon and start walking. It's only a matter of where and when.

Just moments after I think about ditching the bike, the little engine on my Triumph starts to sputter. It sputters for a just a few seconds…and then the engine quits. Looks like the decision of where to ditch the bike isn't mine to make; the bike just made it for me. I coast the bike to the side of the road in front of a two-story building of some kind, extend the kickstand, and climb off. I pick Maggie up from the bike seat and set her down on her feet beside me.

"We'll have to walk from here," I say. "We're out of gas."

"I'm cold," she says.

I look down at her and see that she is shivering uncontrollably. It's cold out and all of that wind blowing on her has probably chilled her to the core. I lean down, embrace her, and hold her body tight against mine to try to warm her up.

I continue to hold her body against mine and after several minutes her body stops shaking. I release my embrace and look into her eyes while crouched down in front of her.

"Feel better now?" I ask.

Maggie sniffles loudly and then nods her head up and down.

"Do you think you can do some walking?"

She nods her head up and down again while clutching Carrie Anne tightly to her chest.

"Okay, let's go."

I stand up and start walking toward the city. I hear the shuffle of little feet beside me. A dog barks somewhere in the distance. We are quickly running out of daylight and I know I'll have to find shelter for both of us very soon. We don't need much; just a simple place to sleep will do fine. Maggie and I are both used to making do with very little. I start scanning my surroundings for a good place to rest for the night.

I feel something take hold of my hand. I look down and see Maggie's hand in mine. I give her hand a little squeeze and continue holding it as we walk. I now see this little girl for who she really is. She's not some monster who was going to eat me, but rather, she's just a scared and confused little girl who was being manipulated by that man… whoever he was. It suddenly occurs to me that Maggie doesn't even look anything like him. I'm starting to have doubts that he really was her father.

I look down at Maggie again and she looks up to me with a look of trust. I give her a little smile and then turn my attention back to looking for a place to stay tonight.

"Don't move another step!" I hear from behind me in a loud voice.

I freeze and a cold chill courses through my body. I look down at Maggie and see a look of confusion and fear on her face. *Surely I haven't come this far just to be delivered right into the hands of the sentries,* I wonder.

"Don't make any sudden movements," I say to Maggie. "Let me do all the talking." She continues to look at me with the same expression and doesn't say anything.

"Turn around slowly," the distorted voice behind me says.

I let go of Maggie's hand and slowly turn around. Before me is a fully exposed Detroit sentry, but something's odd about the scene in front of me. The sentry is much shorter than all of the others I've seen, and it's unarmed, too. It isn't even carrying a police baton.

The sentry walks up to me and looks me over carefully through its helmet visor.

"Don't move, Adam Reese!" the sentry says. "You're a wanted man for what you did."

I say nothing in reply.

In the distance I see a blur, a distortion in my field of view, and then another Detroit sentry appears. The second sentry starts walking toward me. He's clearly taller than the first, and he's not armed, either.

"Don't move!" the first sentry says as the second one approaches.

"What have we got here?" the taller sentry asks.

"Something you lost," the shorter sentry says.

"So I see," the taller sentry says. "So I see."

The taller sentry looks me over through his visor, just as the shorter one did a moment ago.

"Both of you, into that alley," the taller sentry says and nods in the direction of a side alley between two buildings.

I take Maggie's hand and we both walk into the alley. If they start beating me or if they intend on killing me right here, I'll tell Maggie to run. I doubt they'll be interested in her anyway. I don't know where she'll run to or what her fate will be, but at least she'll have a chance, which is more than I can say for myself.

"That's far enough," one of the sentries says. "Now turn around."

So, this is it, I think. *This is how it all ends for me.* I stop walking, let go of Maggie's hand, and slowly turn around. And then I gasp in surprise at what I see before me.

The taller sentry is no longer wearing his helmet and I recognize the face that just a moment ago was hidden behind a mask.

"You've missed all the fun," Dr. Bradshaw says while holding the sentry helmet in one of his arms. "Elise and I were just exploring the suits' capabilities. Amazing, simply amazing!"

I let out a loud sigh of relief. I try to respond to him but I can't formulate any words. It's as though the shock is so great that it renders my brain incapable of speech.

The shorter sentry reaches up, disconnects the data and power cable connecting the suit to the helmet and then lifts the helmet with both hands, revealing Elise.

"Who's your new friend?" Elise asks.

"This is Maggie," I say. "Maggie, can you say hello to Dr. Bradshaw and Elise?"

"Hello," Maggie says. "Nice to meet you."

"Oh, the pleasure is ours," Dr. Bradshaw says as he reaches down and shakes Maggie's hand.

"Hi, Maggie," Elise says as she winks at her.

"Adam, we need to get you acclimated to the suit," Dr. Bradshaw says.

"Me?" I say.

"Yes, you. You and I are about the same size so you should fit the suit I'm wearing."

"You aren't going to—"

"Oh, I'm much too old for anything like that," Dr. Bradshaw says. "And I need to stay behind and take care of the sick and injured anyway. Now, we should all get going. We don't need to be out in the open any longer than we have to. And we don't have much time to prepare anyway."

Dr. Bradshaw pats me on the back. "Our first attack is tomorrow," he says. "You're leading it."

The Detroitopia saga continues!

Be sure to check out the next installment, Unforeseen Consequences, to see what happens next!

www.ingramcontent.com/pod-product-compliance
Lightning Source LLC
Chambersburg PA
CBHW030637130626
46552CB00002B/897